The Scandalous Mrs. Wilson

LAINE FERNDALE

Crimson Romance

New York   London   Toronto   Sydney   New Delhi

CRIMSON
ROMANCE
Crimson Romance
An Imprint of Simon & Schuster, Inc.
1230 Avenue of the Americas
New York, NY 10020

First Crimson Romance e-book edition MAY 2017

CRIMSON ROMANCE and colophon are trademarks of Simon and Schuster.

For information about special discounts for bulk purchases, please contact Simon & Schuster Special Sales at 1-866-506-1949 or business@simonandschuster.com.

The Simon & Schuster Speakers Bureau can bring authors to your live event. For more information or to book an event contact the Simon & Schuster Speakers Bureau at 1-866-248-3049 or visit our website at www.simonspeakers.com.

Manufactured in the United States of America

10 9 8 7 6 5 4 3 2 1

Library of Congress Cataloging-in-Publication Data has been applied for.

ISBN 978-1-5072-0624-9
ISBN 978-1-5072-0478-8 (ebook)

Part 1

Chapter 1

If Fraser Springs held a dirty looks contest, Mrs. McSheen would be the reigning champion. Josephine Wilson swept the wooden planks of the bathhouse's porch as she considered the list of other likely entrants. Mrs. McSheen would face stiff competition from the ladies of the First Presbyterian congregation, the Ladies' Charitable Club, and the Society for the Advancement of Moral Temperance. World-class scowlers, every one. There were probably more societies in this tiny town than there were ladies to fill them. Heavens knew how they found the time to play bridge in between all of the meetings.

It was a beautiful morning. The sharp, mineral tang of the springs felt invigorating in the breeze, not oppressive as it could on a hotter day. The rhododendrons in front of the bathhouse were fat and rosy. There was no reason for scowls. But Mrs. McSheen was intent on showing little Emma McSheen, dressed in a starched white pinafore with a pink sash, how a true lady treats a woman like Josephine.

"Can ... *may* I have a flower?" little Emma asked.

"Any flower grown from this soil is not fit for good little girls such as yourself, dearest," Mrs. McSheen said, proffering Josephine another of her world-famous sneers as she clomped down the wooden boardwalk towards the general store. "And at any rate, those gaudy red things smell like cheap perfume."

In the years since her husband died and she took over the bathhouse, Josephine had received more dirty looks than she could count. Scowls, muttered curses, raised eyebrows; someone had even gone so far as to throw a rock through one of her windows. Mostly, however, the townspeople's outrage took the form of anonymous letters slipped under her door or left in her mailbox. She was a whore, apparently. A harlot. A murderess. A temptress. A jezebel. A "shrew sent from the environs of hell to cast ruin and immorality upon the weak." (It was clear Fraser Springs had at least one aspiring poet among its citizens.) She called them her love letters and kept them all tied with a red ribbon in the top corner of her husband's old desk as a daily reminder of how important it was to maintain a thick skin.

But the hot springs looked lovely today. The surface roiled in shades of silver, purple, and blue. Mist swirled in tendrils towards the rocky shore of the lake, and somehow its color made her think of opals. Josephine had never actually seen an opal, but with the hot springs reflecting the sun into pools of light on the boardwalk, it wasn't hard to imagine. After each day's work ended, there wasn't much to do in Fraser Springs besides imagine.

The town was little more than a cluster of wood-framed houses huddled around its namesake hot spring, the rickety structures leaning towards the water like old hens huddling together for warmth. In recent years, a few lucky mining operations and health-seeking tourists had provided the money for a fancy brick bank and the St. Alice Hotel with its marble floors and formal dining room. It was a town at a crossroads, and it was clear which way Mrs. McSheen and her cronies wanted it to go. The improvements had drawn a whole class of respectable women intent on scrubbing out the traces of the Canadian wilderness. Never mind that the town was a seven-hour steamboat ride from Vancouver or that their closest neighbours were bears or that the main patrons of the springs' bathhouses were still loggers and miners hoping to soothe a year's worth of aches and injuries.

"Miz Jo, customer!" Ilsa's call drew Josephine out of her daydreaming. She'd poached Ilsa from a dance hall in Gastown, but though she was no longer earning her living by charming men into buying overpriced drinks, no amount of training could rid her of her sultry voice. She could make an advertisement for dentures sound like a provocation.

When Josephine's husband had passed away suddenly, the staff he'd spent a lifetime cultivating had taken the next boat back to Vancouver. She had been faced with a choice: close the bathhouse or find new staff as quickly as possible. She'd chosen the latter and assembled a cadre of equally desperate women who she'd trained in the healing art of massage—and massage only. The women were quick learners and keen to start new lives, and the lure of an all-female staff had paid off. Soon, Wilson's Bathhouse had become so successful that the husbands of the Society Ladies started becoming patrons. Now, however, business was down, and nasty letters were the order of the day.

Jo propped the broom against the wall, pulled off her apron, and tucked a stray curl back into her chignon. Whatever the McSheens of this town might think, her customers would meet a polished and respectable proprietress when they arrived.

She took a breath and straightened her posture. There, that was better. In a business like this, you never knew who was going to be on the other side of the door: maybe an old miner, maybe a local businessman who'd snuck in through the side entrance to avoid suspicion. Either way, Jo was ready.

• • •

Owen Sterling sat in one of the overstuffed chairs of Wilson's Bathhouse. Did the bowler hat look ridiculous? It was on loan from his publisher, as was the gold pocket watch and the three-piece suit, but it was important to look the part. In his Vancouver bachelor quarters, he'd dressed carefully and practiced introducing himself.

"Why hello there," he'd told the mirror as he'd slicked back his hair with pomade and parted it. "My name is Ross Wister. It is a pleasure to meet you." Ross Wister, wealthy banker, not Owen Sterling, writer of wilderness stories, soon-to-be ace reporter.

When he broke this story, he wouldn't be stuck writing about boys, their loyal canine companions, and the increasingly unlikely capers in which they found themselves. He'd be a real journalist, writing about real people and issues that really mattered. And so for now, he had to be Ross Wister, a banker with a nervous condition in need of the "services" of Wilson's Bathhouse.

Owen stared out through the plate glass window and tried to focus on the hot springs in the distance to keep himself from fidgeting. The window had *Wilson's* written across it in gold lettering and was adorned with dozens of blue bottles hung from fishing line. The bottles tinkled melodically as they swayed against one another, and the mottled blue light they cast made him feel as if he were underwater. The sales cases along the walls were full of more blue bottles, together with tins that seemed to be filled with poultices and powders. Snake oil. The selling of false cures to desperate people was disgusting, but not nearly as disgusting as what his publisher had assured him was going on behind closed doors.

"It's a house of ill repute, and they don't even try to hide it," his publisher had said. "I've got several trustworthy sources who tell me that Joe Wilson hires thugs to kidnap innocent farm girls, then keeps them trapped in a life of sin. One day they're in their parents' loving home, and the next, they're earning their keep in a brothel. One big article exposing Joe Wilson, and the whole operation will be run out of town. They say Joe Wilson's a murderer, too. How's that for a story for you?"

A door opened quietly behind him. Owen looked up.

"How can I help you?" asked the slim figure standing just inside the doorway. Bold as brass, especially after he'd specifically requested to speak to Joe Wilson, not another of his "lady attendants." For a fallen woman, though, she looked surprisingly wholesome and respectable: auburn hair pulled into a proper chignon, modestly dressed in a neatly pressed white shirtwaist and bottle-blue skirts. Her eyes, flinty and pale grey, were the only hint that this woman was no stranger to the ways of the world. He could sense her sizing him up, probably calculating his annual salary.

He stood, determined to act the gentleman. "I specifically told your ... colleague that I want to speak to Mr. Joe Wilson," he said. "I have business with him."

The woman's mouth quirked just a little. Not a smirk, exactly, but unsettling enough. "Oh you do, do you?"

"I most certainly do. And I do not appreciate being kept waiting." That sounded like the way a banker would talk. He ran his thumb over the embossed face of the pocket watch in his waistcoat pocket. The metal was slick under his palm. He wasn't sure if it was the wool suit, the bowler, or the woman's appraising look, but he was beginning to sweat.

The woman put a hand on her hip, her eyes narrowing. "Ah. I hate to disappoint you, but you ought to know that the Joe Wilson you have business with is actually Mrs. Josephine Wilson." She walked few steps forward, and Owen caught the faint, warm odour of talc. "My late husband was Albert Wilson, founder and proprietor and so on."

No banker's bluster could hide Owen's confusion. "Oh, I ... I'm sorry, I thought you were a ..."

Jo Wilson's smile seemed slightly chagrined. That was a little comforting, perhaps. Her voice, however, was even. "I'm terribly sorry to disappoint you, Mr. ...?" She paused expectantly.

Owen wrapped himself in the protective dignity of his phony persona, extended his hand, and gave the name he'd been practicing for so long. "My name is Ross Wister. It's a pleasure to meet you, ma'am."

When she shook his hand, he found himself staring into those grey eyes, so pale they were almost colourless. Her hand, warm and faintly rough, sent a chill through him. "You as well," she said in her carefully even voice. "What can we do for you, Mr. Wister?" And she smiled again.

Mister Wister. How had he not heard that absurd sing-songy rhyme when he'd chosen the name? Damn. Owen shoved his hand back in his pocket, pulled out the pocket watch, and burnished it against his trouser leg. "I've been advised by my physician that the stresses of banking have grown too much for me. I've been plagued by headaches and fatigue. Neurasthenia, the doctor says."

Her smile remained fixed and professional. This irked him, for some reason. "I'm sorry to hear that. I suppose overwork must be a hazard of your profession, Mr. Wister."

"He tells me that a stay at the hot springs are just what I need to restore my constitution. And I've heard that Wilson's is the best."

Jo's expression softened, the smile becoming a bit more sincere. The sun through the plate glass window lit her hair in shades of copper. It was distracting, but Owen forced himself to meet her gaze again. Notorious madams did not have lovely copper-colored hair.

"We most certainly are very good," she said. "Let me bring you a list of our treatments. Will you be staying in our cabins?" Unlike the thoroughly modern accommodations at the St. Alice, guests at Wilson's Bathhouse boarded in the clapboard cabins behind the main building, with meals served from the bathhouse's kitchen.

"Uh, no, thank you. That is, I've taken rooms elsewhere. But I'll take my meals here, if that's possible."

Jo nodded. "Of course. I'll be happy to arrange that for you."

She retrieved a ledger from the counter and came to sit on the chair beside him. "Have a seat, please, and we'll get you sorted."

Underneath her talc scent, she smelled of grass and leaves rather than the heavy perfumes he'd expect from a woman in her line of work. Probably whatever she'd been crushing to put into these snake oil cures. Eye of newt, toe of frog, and what have you.

"For headaches, I would recommend our standard bath, with our salve treatment and a mercury tincture to relieve tension and anxiety." Salve treatment! One salve treatment delivered by one of these young ladies would be the start of a very successful exposé. He'd get to the bottom of what was really going on at Wilson's Bathhouse inside of a week. Three days, if he was half the journalist he knew he was.

Chapter 2

The stranger with the borrowed suit wasn't fooling her. Not for a single moment. For starters, he was too handsome: strikingly so. The loose fit of that sack suit couldn't hide his strong shoulders. His blue eyes were startlingly alert, and though his jawline betrayed tension, it surely wasn't the result of balancing account ledgers and foreclosing on penniless widows. Besides, anyone with a suit that fine would be walking his fancy shoes straight over to the St. Alice's marble foyer, not into Wilson's, with its arthritic miners and battered loggers and slightly tarnished reputation. Yet he hadn't blinked as she'd signed him on for every service Wilson's offered, and he'd calmly nodded when she'd asked for a truly absurd deposit and he'd placed the notes into her hand with that same unnerving blue glitter in his eyes. Something was most definitely amiss.

"Don't see a fellow like that around here often," Ilsa said when Jo joined her to help crush mint leaves for salves. "Almost makes me wish this *was* a house of ill repute!"

"Well, it's not," Jo snapped. "And it's not going to be. I'd lay odds that that man is here with ulterior motives."

"Do you think he has strange tastes, then?" Ilsa whispered, delighted. Her eyes were wide. Ilsa had hair so blond it looked almost white, and eyes so blue that men were forever writing her poetry comparing them to the water and the sky. Which showed what men knew, since Ilsa was as earthy as anything in God's creation.

Jo dug the pestle into her mortar. "He might. You never know, though I suspect he's too bad a liar to have lived a life of perversion. Still, it's strange." The mint leaves released their oils against the stone bowl, and she breathed in the clean, cool scent. She leaned her weight into her work. "In fact, schedule his treatments with me. I don't want any of the girls around him until I know what he's up to."

Ilsa laughed. She had a high, giggling laugh that sounded younger than her nineteen years. "Oh sure," she said. "First good-looking rich man comes through here, and you want him all to yourself. Girls aren't going to be too happy with that."

Jo shook her head. "I've got problems enough without throwing myself at men. He's after something. I'll take care of his treatments, and we'll see what it is. Tell the girls to give him a wide berth."

Ilsa laughed again. "Good luck with that. The mint, Miz Jo." Jo looked down to discover that she'd smashed the poor leaves to an absolute pulp.

Their laughter was interrupted by Doc Stryker slamming open the kitchen's screen door. Doc owned the establishment next door, which apparently made him too important to knock like a civilized neighbor. His leaflets claimed that he was a doctor shunned by the medical profession for discovering the key to eternal youth, but it didn't take a genius to suspect that his medical license was more than likely purchased from some ad in the back of a mail-order catalog. Doc's premises featured a menu of eye-watering "restorative libations," and the card and dice games that went on in back of the bar were the worst kept secret in Fraser Springs.

"Good morning, Doc," Jo said.

"They're threatening us," he replied by way of greeting. His face was so pale you could see the blue veins underneath his temples as he waved a crumpled piece of paper at her. Jo took it from him, feeling the trembling of his fingers.

"They've been posting this around town," he said. "Puttin' one on every fence post, handing them out to the tourists. They're coming for us."

She smoothed out the paper. Unlike the other handmade signs, this one had been properly typeset.

To all Good Citizens of Fraser Springs:

There is a Great Menace lurking among us, and We all Know what it is. We have been blessed with a Miracle from God in our Town: Waters that Restore Energy and Give Health. That Cure the Sick and the Wounded. If We want the Good and Proper Citizens to enjoy the many benefits of our Miracle Waters, We must rid them of Corruption.

Every Good Citizen knows that there are certain Dens of Ill Repute that infest our town with Filth, Drunkenness, Gambling, and Sins of the Flesh. We, the Society for the Advancement of Moral Temperance, call for a meeting of all True Citizens of Fraser Springs. Come to the St. Alice Hotel on Saturday at noon, and We will decide on the Fate of the Town together. Our Town is at a Crossroads, Ladies and Gentlemen. Make no mistake. Will it be dragged into Squalor and Filth, or will it Rise Greater than Vancouver or even New York City? Let us commit to Rise and never to Fall.

Yours in Christ,

The Society for the Advancement of Moral Temperance

Jo pressed her hand against the small of her back to hide the tremor that rushed through her. Bits and pieces of this declaration had already slid under her front door or sailed through her window.

"They're going to run us out of here," Doc said. "It's a land grab! That's what this is about. We've got the best land. The best view of the springs. Step out your front door, and you've got the springs right at your feet. Even if a man can't hardly walk, he can take a few steps off your front porch and be in the water." The salesman's patter came so easily to Doc he barely seemed to notice that he'd slipped into his pitch. "You get them healthy vapours from the minerals while you're sleeping if you keep your window open." He paused, seemed to recollect himself. "Your place, Jo. You've got the springs out the front and then more in back, past the trails and the cabins. They want our land."

"That's as may be. They can't have it."

"They're going to take it. Just snatch it! Sin and temperance—phaw! Who do you think comes to my table every night? Who do you think spends the money? And Mrs. McSheen's husband's the worst of the lot! She's probably sore because he lost her silver teapot in a game of stud poker last Saturday." The little man turned from white to red as he began pacing around the foyer as if on a stage, almost bursting out of his tweed waistcoat. "Hypocrites, the lot of them. Sin and vice, they say? Your girls don't do nothing but give the same treatments everyone else here does; they just look prettier while doing it. No two bones about it. Only sin is the evil looks those Society women give out. Cold, unchristian shrews."

"Just settle down. They're not going to take anything, Doc. Ilsa, fetch him a glass of water." Jo led him towards the sofa and sat him down.

"Damned McSheen woman's kettle ain't even real silver. Just cheap plate," he muttered sullenly.

"They can't take our land. They're just bored women who want a project. There's no war to wind bandages for, and a body can only stitch so many samplers. They've got to do something with their days."

Doc didn't smile. He was staring straight ahead, out towards the hot springs. "This is different. I can feel it."

She put a hand on his shoulder. "It's going to be fine. We go to the meeting and we speak our piece. They'll shake their Bibles and show off for each other, and everyone will go home and pat themselves on the back for having saved the town."

Doc grabbed the hand that was on his shoulder and held it. "You're young, Jo. But I'm old. I've been run out of towns before. Was with the circus before I got into this game. Nothing on stage, just moving the animals around, though I guess I would make a pretty good bearded lady." He stroked his beard and pretended to bat his eyelashes at Ilsa, who giggled as she passed him the glass of water. "But I know what it feels like to be on the receiving end of an angry crowd; let's just say that." He took a long swig of his water and set the glass down.

Jo didn't feel young. She'd come to town with her father when she was just seventeen. No one knew what had sickened him, but the rumour was that Fraser Springs could cure what ailed any man. They'd come from Calgary and taken the train through the Crowsnest Pass, where she'd been dazzled by the greenery and the mountains, by the sheer height of everything. And then her father—no, she didn't want to think of it. She'd married Albert, and he'd died less than a year into their marriage, and now she was the proprietress of the bathhouse that bore his name.

"They've got no reason to run us out," she said. "We haven't done anything wrong."

A banging door reminded them both that customers would soon be wandering in for the noon meal, and Doc stood to go. Ilsa rushed to begin setting the tables. But before Doc left, he leaned in, his mouth set in a hard line. "Angry crowd don't need a reason, Jo. Remember that."

Chapter 3

Later that evening, inside his room at the ornate St. Alice Hotel, Owen breathed a sigh of relief. Despite the early stumble, he'd pulled it off. She couldn't suspect a thing. Nice of his sorry excuse for a publisher to neglect to tell him that Joe Wilson was a she, and an attractive she at that! He put it out of his mind. Hard to find a woman attractive when you knew she was spiriting young girls away from their homes to work in sin.

It didn't take his investigative prowess to see that the St. Alice looked more like the front parlor of a brothel than Wilson's. The windows were decked out in red velour curtains. The bed had a red velour coverlet and pillows with gold braid tassels. More velour and tassels on the tablecloth draped over the suggestively curving legs of the dressing table. The yards of heavy fabric seemed to suffocate him. Still, he stretched out on the four-poster bed, intending to take mental notes on his first encounter.

Owen sat back up almost immediately. The mattress had entirely too much give for a man used to spending months at a time sleeping on the ground, and the sinking sensation was unpleasant.

It didn't feel right to use his publisher's money for this ridiculous room, but every real journalist he knew had an expense account for investigative work. And besides, when he broke this story and those poor, trapped girls were returned to their families, the money would have been well spent. There would be a boost in his reputation as a writer, maybe even reprints in national magazines.

Owen strode to the window, opened it, and took a breath of the humid, faintly sulfuric air. It was a welcome change from the room's stuffy odour of beeswax and rosewater. No science aficionado worth his salt would believe that hot springs could heal, but the smell was at least bracing. It was an honest, unfussy, outdoors odour, and he liked it. Since coming to Vancouver in the spring of 1894, he'd been on many expeditions into the wilderness, gathering inspiration for his series of boys' own adventure stories, but he'd never come so far up the coast.

The sun was finally setting, and only a small sliver of moon would be out. Time to get some real work started in this investigation. It stood to reason that in a small town like this, most of the action at a brothel would happen under the cover of darkness. There was no time to waste. In a burst of renewed energy, he removed the three-piece suit and put on his own clothes: a round-collared shirt, sturdy slacks, and an old knit cardigan. He stuffed his notebook in his pocket.

In the St. Alice's marble-floored lobby, a group of fussily dressed ladies stood gossiping in a tight knot. He drifted near and pretended to inspect a basket of wax fruit sitting on a pedestal.

"The McMillans are with us, as are the Waltons and the Drummonds. All the best families are fully committed," one woman whispered.

"Well, of course they are," another woman cooed. "Who else are they going to side with? Mr. Stryker? That murdering temptress?"

Could they mean Jo Wilson? Were the townsfolk finally taking matters into their own hands?

"Where's your husband anyhow? Didn't you say he was coming?" asked a third.

"Oh," said the first one, waving the question away as she suddenly noticed Owen's eavesdropping. "Working, I'm sure. There's so much new business coming in that he probably lost track of time. Shall we begin with a Scripture reading in the parlour?"

Not wanting to arouse suspicion, Owen headed outside into the cool air, following the creaking boardwalk that wound around the perimeter of the springs towards Wilson's. Even in the dark, he could feel the warm mist coming off the water. Beyond, a few lights dotted the hillside —miners' cabins, probably—but otherwise, it was oppressively dark. Owen went slowly to avoid falling off the boardwalk. You'd think the town would have sprung for some lamps along with the fancy hotel and the bank.

Once he neared Wilson's, he left the noisy boardwalk and slowly picked his way through the rocky outcroppings that led up to the building's front porch. The plate glass window blazed with light, and a phonograph's tinny music came from somewhere inside. Owen ducked along the side of the main house, hoping that the music would overpower the sound of gravel crunching beneath his feet.

Inside, he heard voices: two women, it sounded like. He couldn't hear what they were saying, so he inched closer along the wall, avoiding the swath of light the window cut. Still, the music muffled their voices. Could he hear men? It was hard to tell ...

"Stop right where you are," came a voice behind him.

He whirled around. Jo Wilson stood not three feet away, with an ancient hunting rifle at her shoulder.

"Don't shoot, Mrs. Wilson," he blurted, holding up his hands. "It's just me. I'm not armed."

"Wister. What are you doing sneaking around here? Hoping to peek at some girls undressing?" She took a step closer, and the rifle's barrel was only a few inches from his chest.

"Of course not! I got lost! I was trying to find my way back from the lake."

She lowered the rifle slightly. The lantern light added a bronze sheen to her auburn hair. Her grey eyes looked brighter in the light. *Gun. Focus on the rifle, not the lady holding it.*

"Where are you staying?"

"The, uh, St. Alice."

Jo raised the gun again. "The St. Alice! If you're staying in that marble monstrosity, what are you doing even taking treatments at my place? Why don't you soak in their fancy baths? What are you doing here?"

"I'm lost! And, besides, I was told your bathhouse is the best." Luckily, the cover of darkness hid his blush. He couldn't very well say he was a journalist, but he also didn't enjoy implying that he was on the prowl for ladies of ill repute.

Jo leaned towards him. "If you're looking for the St. Alice, allow me to give you a hint. Just look for the only large structure within a hundred miles, with enough electric lights to be seen from the heavens. Literally the only bright thing in all these miles of darkness." She swept her hand wide, gesturing over the rocks and the boardwalk towards the St. Alice. The hotel's illuminated windows cast a wavering glow over the lake. She stared intently at him. "I've met men like you before, getting your little thrills by sneaking up on women. Peeping Toms."

"I am most certainly not a Peeping Tom! Good Lord, do you speak to all of your customers this way?"

"Only the ones I find creeping around my property after hours."

"I'm sorry. I've had a little too much to drink, and I was all turned around. I'm not used to this darkness. And I heard music: I thought you might be having a party."

"Ha! I know what kind of 'party' you were looking for. I told you before. We're a respectable house. It's just my staff and myself in there. Which you knew, because you were peeping through the windows."

"I wasn't peeping! And could you please point that gun somewhere other than at my person? I'm not Jack the Ripper."

"How do I know that?"

Slowly, he reached towards the barrel of the gun. She looked uncertain, but her finger moved off the trigger. He pushed the barrel to one side, moving slowly and deliberately, as if she were a wild creature he'd startled in its den. "Because I'm just lost. I wasn't trying to do whatever it is you're accusing me of doing. I got turned around. I'm sorry."

"Well, you're new here," she said, finally. "But don't even so much as talk to my girls when you come in tomorrow."

Owen nodded, putting up both hands to show that he meant no harm. "Understood," he said. He took a few steps backwards. "Have a good night, Mrs. Wilson. I'm sorry about the mix-up."

She didn't respond. Confident that she was no longer going to shoot him, he turned tail and headed back for the safety of the boardwalk. Though he did not dare to look back, he could feel those grey eyes watching him in the dark.

•••

Jo slammed the door behind her, startling Ilsa, who was still scrubbing potatoes for the morning breakfast as she swayed to the love song on the phonograph. Jo's heart was beating so hard it made her limbs buzz.

"Where did you run off to so fast?" Ilsa asked, wiping her forehead and leaving a smudge of dirt there. "And what are you doing with the gun?"

Jo fixed the safety, propped the gun against the wall, and began pulling all of the curtains shut. "Just saying hello to our newest customer. I heard a noise and thought it was the Temperance Society come to deliver me one of their little love letters. I found Mr. Wister sneaking around, trying to spy on us"

Ilsa came to help her. "What was he looking for?"

"He said he was lost. How can you get lost looking for the St. Alice?"

"He's staying there? Why isn't he getting his treatments at their place? And now to be prowling around here like the cat around hot porridge ..." Ilsa's Scandinavian idioms came out at odd times.

Jo steadied herself against the back of the chair. Maybe it was the looming town meeting, but the encounter with Mr. Wister had left her rattled. Perhaps he had been hired by the Temperance Society to spy on them. Or maybe he'd come slumming around her bathhouse to rid himself of unclean urges that he couldn't indulge at the St. Alice. Even in the dim light of the lantern, she could tell that he'd been too calm by half for a disoriented city banker at the wrong end of a rifle.

"I don't know. It's all very suspicious. Be careful tonight, Ilsa. If you hear anything, come get me."

Jo slept that night with the gun leaned against the foot of the bed, as she had in the first months after Albert's passing. She heard everything acutely: the springs fizzling beneath her window, the pines rustling against one another, the dogs (or were they wolves?) howling in the mountains. If she could manage being orphaned at seventeen in a strange town, followed by a hasty marriage and the passing of her new husband—all within less than a year—and if she could somehow turn a profit on this tumbledown bathhouse in spite of women who spent their evenings praying for guidance on how best to ruin her ... Well, she and her girls could manage Ross Wister just fine.

Chapter 4

Burning with embarrassment, Owen could only trudge back the way he'd come in the darkness. Less than a day gone, and his investigation was already a shambles. Maybe he'd been deluding himself all along. Maybe all he was good for was writing stories about loyal huskies and their improbably heroic twelve-year-old owners.

The quiet of Fraser Springs was broken by boisterous voices spilling out from a bathhouse built half on the shore of the hot springs and half on stilts jutting into the water. Three signs tacked onto the porch posts read Doc Stryker's, Every Ailment and Complaint Cured, and All Are Welcome. Well, Owen surely needed a cure for everything right then.

Inside, he was greeted with a blast of stale alcohol fumes. Cigar smoke mingled with wood smoke from a small stove burning at the back of the bar. Clustered around low tables, men dealt cards and argued, while a solid little man with a tidy white beard and tiny round glasses strolled between the tables, his two hands tapping on his belly like a king surveying his lands.

Owen took a seat at the bar beside a young man wearing a neatly patched plaid coat.

"Evenin'," said the man, only barely glancing in his direction.

"Evenin'," Owen said, too tired to even begin to pull together the appropriate small talk. He waited for the man to strike up a conversation, but he remained hunched over his sketchbook.

Owen drummed his fingers. "Drawing something?" he asked finally.

The man's obvious first instinct was to bring his arm protectively around his drawing, but he checked himself and showed Owen his sketch. "Just this fellow here." He pointed to an upside-down whiskey glass on the bar. Owen leaned in and saw, underneath the glass, a small, gray, oblong creature trundling along in circles around the scarred wood of the bar top.

"A pill bug?" The drawing was actually quite good. The man had taken great care shading the creature's armour so that it looked almost mechanical.

The man sighed. "Armadillidiidae. Or, more specifically, *Armadillidium vulgare*. Did you know that they're actually crustaceans? Like lobsters?" He flipped over the glass and nudged the little bug with the tip of his pencil. It rolled up into a ball. "Closest you get to lobsters up here." The man had a faint, musically lilting accent. Danish or Swedish, for sure.

"Are you some kind of naturalist?" Owen asked.

"Naw, just a trapper." He wiped his hand's graphite smudges on his pants and extended it. "Nils Barson. This," he gestured to the sketchbook, "is only a hobby. Got my hands on a few books when I was a boy, and I've been at it ever since. You'd be surprised, you know, about Fraser Springs. What with the mineral springs, you see every manner of creature."

"I bet," Owen said. "I'm Ross Wister."

Despite Nils's rugged attire, he had the pink cheeks and blond stubble of a younger man. His dark blond curls, which he'd made no effort to shear into a grown man's haircut, made him look no older than twenty. "So not from around here, then. What brings you to Fraser Springs?" An argument flared up around a card game, and both men turned to look. Nothing serious. When Owen looked back at the bar, the pill bug had wandered off to parts unknown.

"Doctor recommended a few weeks in the hot springs to cure some ills. Thought I'd relax, see the ... you know, sights." He gave Nils a knowing leer to encourage the man on to the subject of Wilson's Bathhouse and the sights one might find there.

"A little time in the timber would do any man good," Nils said, smoothing the edge of his drawing. "And the springs are nice. Can't say they've ever cured me of anything, but they are restful."

The barkeep came by and Owen ordered a whiskey. "And one for my friend here," he said. The barkeep poured two generous drinks from a ceramic jar and placed them in front of the men. Owen raised the drink to his lips. Little bits of sediment were suspended in the liquid. It tasted of moss and kerosene. The alcohol (what kind, he couldn't say) burned down his throat and fanned into a warmth in his stomach, making a merciful start on scalding away this embarrassment of an evening.

Nils nodded his thanks. "Cheers," he said. He downed the drink in one gulp, and the barkeep refilled their glasses. "I mostly come here for the light—cheaper to buy a few drinks than to waste lamp fuel in my own place—but I guess a little company don't hurt."

"Good to talk to a new face," Owen said. "You live in town?"

"Naw. I got a little cabin up in the hills there. City life doesn't interest me much."

City life. Owen tried not to snort. "How do you find your way in the dark? I damn near broke my neck trying to feel my way around tonight."

Nils shrugged. "You get used to it." The barkeep refilled their glasses. Nils nodded his thanks again and downed the drink. Owen followed suit, though he was already feeling the effects of the first drink. These townspeople could certainly hold their liquor. But even if half of his per diem money went to loosening the tongues of the locals, it would be worth it. And how much could this cheap swill cost?

"Tell me," Owen said. "What's there to do for fun here? Beyond sitting in hot water and drinking."

"Oh, plenty. Good hunting most of the year. Perch and crappie if you get farther out on the lake. Nice views from the peaks, if you go in for that kind of thing. Do you like to read?"

"I suppose. Sure."

Nils rustled through an oilcloth rucksack at his feet and pulled out a battered paperback book. "Have you read any of these adventure stories? They're all by the same fellow. Whenever I'm feeling low, one of these picks me up. This one's about a boy, right? And he's got this dog, Trigger, and they used to live in a place like this. But he's got no family, so they head out into the wilderness to make their fortune. And one day the boy runs afoul of this evil trapper ..." This was all sounding very familiar. "The trapper doesn't want anyone on his land, right? And ... well, I won't ruin it for you. But it's very exciting."

Owen took the book. On the cover, a boy stood with a rifle and a dog, staring at a mountain range. Below, in large block letters: Owen Sterling. Truthfully, most of his book covers were a variation on that theme: boy and dog staring at sunset. Boy and dog staring at tundra. Boy and dog staring at rocky coastline. "*Escape from Snowy Mountain*," he read.

"I won't give it away, but I did like the part about the mountain. Owen Sterling's my favourite author." Owen tried to hide his smile behind his whiskey dram. He didn't think anyone over the age of fourteen read his work, let alone actual mountain men. "Well, him and Bill Woodson, but Sterling writes the dogs better." Bill Woodson was a pompous windbag who was never seen without the pith helmet he claimed to have gotten on safari in Africa.

"Isn't this stuff just for kids?" Owen asked.

"What? No!" Nils grabbed the book back and opened it to a page. "No, listen to this:

They claimed the Eskimos had thirty-seven words for snow, but even those words wouldn't be enough to describe the fierce blizzard swirling in great, hoary gusts around Danny, threatening to blow him clean off the mountainside and smash him to ruins on the jagged rocks below. The wind howled around the mountain's crevices like a wounded beast. Danny's chill reached beyond his bones into the very marrow. Throughout it all, the noble Trigger stayed surefooted, barking when he uncovered the trail through the storm.

"Now that's some writing right there. I love a story with a dog in it."

"I met Owen Sterling once," Owen said. "In Vancouver. They say he researches his books by going out into the wilderness for months at a time."

Nils looked like a little boy on Christmas morning. "You did? When'd you meet him?"

"He was giving a talk at a club I went to once."

Nils leaned forward, his cheeks flushed with excitement and the cheap hooch. "I can't imagine actually meeting the man. Shaking his hand. I wouldn't think a man like Owen Sterling would have much use for Vancouver."

Even through the blooming haze of the so-called whiskey, Owen had enough of his wits left to stop this conversation before his tongue got any looser. "Maybe I'll borrow that book after all. Give it a read."

"Sure!" Nils said. "I can't believe you met Owen Sterling."

Owen took the book and flipped through it. He knew it was vain, but he could never get tired of seeing his name in print. If this story went well, he would see his name where it mattered most: in the byline of the front page of *The Vancouver World*. He ran his thumb over the gilded letters, then leaned forward. "What do you know about Wilson's Bathhouse? I've got treatments there tomorrow."

"Glad to hear it! You'll see me there. I do handiwork for Mrs. Wilson most days when I'm in town. She feeds me; I hammer what needs to be hammered." He chortled. "Though truth be told, you'd need fifteen of me to get that place back upright. Poor Mrs. Wilson really inherited a mess. Albert was a nice man, but he did tend to let things go."

"Albert was her husband?"

"Yeah, they weren't married long before he took a heart attack. He was only fifty, you know. Young for that kind of trouble, but it just goes to show you, doesn't it?"

"I overheard some folks saying that she killed him." The barkeep returned, pouring them another round. Owen's thoughts were definitely blurring. He needed to get out of Doc's soon, before he really did need help getting back to the St. Alice.

Nils scowled. "Mrs. Wilson wouldn't kill a mad dog. Those women let their imaginations get away from them. That, and they just don't like that she's got those pretty ladies working for her."

"I also heard stories about those pretty ladies," he said, trying to act disinterested through the booze.

But his drinking companion abruptly stood, polished off the last of his drink, and stuffed the sketchbook in his rucksack. "Sorry, but I don't take to gossiping. No offense. I should get back up the mountain before this rotgut has me tumbling over the bluffs. Nice meeting you."

Now that was the reaction of a man with something to hide. Not that Owen blamed him for wanting to protect his employer. "Thanks for the book," he called after Nils, who was already out the door.

Triumphant at last, he threw some coins on the bar and strode out into the dark, carrying the book. People in this town got cagey whenever Jo Wilson was mentioned, but hopefully Doc Stryker's booze had bought him some goodwill with this Nils fellow and would one day loosen his tongue.

Chapter 5

Jo awoke tangled in her sheets, disoriented. All night she'd had fragmented dreams of angry mobs and poison pen letters. That wasn't unusual. What was unusual was how many dreams featured Ross Wister, watching her with those calm blue eyes. They weren't nightmares, exactly. She certainly wasn't afraid of him. He was just there, studying her face with the same slightly bemused expression he'd worn the night before as she'd trained the gun on him in the lantern light. Perhaps she was just curious about him. That seemed like the most likely explanation.

Luckily, the sun was shining this morning. The scent of warm pine needles came off the mountains, and in the early morning stillness, she could already hear people going about their business—joking with one another, tramping down the boardwalk, chopping firewood. It was on days like this that she loved Fraser Springs.

Actually, tree-chopping sounds seemed to be coming from somewhere close to the bathhouse. She stopped to listen. Each sharp thud was accompanied by wild cheers ... from her kitchen? Jo hastily tried to wrestle her hair into some semblance of order, and hustled down the stairs.

It was clear she'd overslept. The girls had breakfast set out on the long slab table: pots of jam, sausages, bread fried brown and glossy with bacon grease, cinnamon rolls, steaming chicory coffee. Miners and loggers in various stages of arthritic decline sat hunched over the plates of food, their suspenders half falling off their shoulders, their knuckles knobby and twisted as they tried to spread jam on their toast. Ilsa and the girls navigated between the men, pouring coffee and carrying plates to and from the tables.

Usually, breakfast was a time of deep quiet as the hungry men tucked into the spread. There was no time for jabbering when fresh bread was on the table. Today, however, all eyes were on a spectacle unfolding in the middle of the dining room. Nils Barson and Mr. Wister were standing side by side, each holding one of her kitchen knives. A log had been dragged in from outside and perched precariously on the cherry credenza. A crude bull's-eye slapped on with red paint was still dripping wet, threatening both the crocheted dresser scarf and her furniture's varnish.

Thwack. Her best butcher's knife jutted out from the center of the bull's-eye, apparently thrown by Mr. Wister. The men cheered, and he gave a proud little bow to the crowd, hamming it up. His sleeves were rolled up and his collar was undone. A few of the girls, clustered by the kitchen door, giggled behind their hands. Jo didn't know many bankers who could boast such excellent aim.

"Your go, Nils," he said. He turned slightly and caught the full blast of her glare. "Oh! Good morning, Mrs. Wilson."

"What are you doing?" All eyes turned to look at her as Jo let loose with both barrels. "What on earth has gotten into you all? Dragging a dirty tree stump into my dining room! Using paint on top of my good furniture. Throwing my *knives*."

As one, the men ducked their heads, looking for all the world like little boys caught playing with matches. "Sorry, Miz Wilson," Nils said, trying to hide his grin. "Mr. Wister was bragging about his skills with a knife, so I had to show him how we do it in Fraser Springs." The men cheered at the mention of their town. "Got to say, though, he's holding his own. We're, uh, tied actually." He looked at Jo, then at the stump, then back at Jo.

Mr. Wister rubbed the back of his neck and avoided her gaze: embarrassed about last night, no doubt. But treating her expensive knives like hatchets was not the most efficient way back into her good graces. "We were just having a bit of fun," he said. "We'll clean everything up."

"Won't take long to set right," said Nils. "Nothing's hurt."

"And how are my knives going to recover from your little stunt?" she asked. "They won't cut butter after you're done. What if you'd missed and thrown a knife through the window?"

Mr. Wister gave her an unabashed grin, his eyes bright with confidence. "Don't worry, ma'am," he said. "I don't miss."

At this, the men roared. "Come on, Miz Wilson," one said. "Can they at least break the tie? I got the last of my pay packet riding on this."

Jo surveyed the scene: the crocheted table runner would need a soaking in bleach, the floor was covered in dirt and bark. How dare Mr. Wister—not to mention Nils—put her in this position? Say no, and she was mean old Mrs. Wilson, spoiling the fun. Say yes, and who knew what other nonsense the men would try to pull. What came after knife throwing? Indoor football? Fire juggling?

"Come on, Miz Jo," Ilsa said, touching her friend's shoulder. "I wouldn't let 'em harm a thing here. And besides," she added more quietly, "I got a coin or two riding on Mr. Wister here."

Everyone in the room looked at her expectantly. She really couldn't win. It wouldn't be long until the Society biddies were accusing her of gambling on top of everything. A little pile of coins, cheap bits of jewelry, and crumpled bills had formed in the center of the front table. The men looked so happy, though, and happy men spent money.

"Fine," she said finally. "But you're cleaning up every last speck of dirt. And sharpening my knives. And if you make so much as a nick in my wall, even God won't be able to save you from—"

Everyone's cheers drowned out her threats.

"Drinks for everyone if I win, lads!" Mr. Wister cried, raising his hands in the air. "And we'll all toast the patience and good nature of Mrs. Wilson."

"Mrs. Wilson!" the men cheered, raising their mugs of chicory as if they were beer.

"Honestly," muttered Jo as she stalked to the back of the room. "Well? Get on with it!"

"This is sudden death, ladies and gentlemen," Mr. Wister announced, removing the knives from the log and handing one to Nils. "One throw each. Nearest to the bull's-eye is the winner, judged by the innermost part of the knife. Mrs. Wilson here can be judge to keep us honest." And he *winked* at her.

"May the best man win," Nils said. She'd never seen Nils so animated. He was usually in a corner drawing and avoiding conversation

"You first," said Mr. Wister, gesturing towards Nils.

Nils placed his toe on the line, squared his shoulders, and tested the heft of a bread knife in his palm. The crowd hushed as he aimed and tossed the knife. *Thwack.* It hit the log less than an inch from dead center. Everyone cheered.

"Attaboy, Nils!" "You show 'im!" came the cries of the miners.

"Not bad," Mr. Wister said. He and Nils inspected the gash left in the log. "Come measure, Mrs. Wilson. You're the judge."

Jo came closer. Mr. Wister ducked down on his haunches next to her. "Now, you've got to measure from the innermost edge of the notch." Someone had fished the measuring tape from her sewing kit and handed it to her. She knelt down to measure, distinctly aware of Mr. Wister's collarless bulk and the crowd behind her.

"Three-quarters of an inch from the bull's-eye. You've got quite a challenge, sir," she said, giving Mr. Wister what she hoped was a lofty, dignified expression.

"He's good," Mr. Wister said. "Now let's see what I can do." He gave her another wink. She stood up and retreated to the back of the room.

"Enough showboating," she said. "Let's wrap this up, gentlemen."

Mr. Wister smiled again. "Just want to give these boys here a few more minutes with their money before I take it from them."

Half the men gave good-natured jeers. Mr. Wister took the butcher's knife and positioned himself at the makeshift throwing line. He made a show of licking his finger and pretending to test the air, drawing a few giggles from the girls who had crowded around the tables to watch. Then, his eyes narrowed as he focused on the log. He took a slow breath, and Jo watched his calm resolve. That must be some nervous condition he had.

Thwack. The butcher's knife hit the log, lodged firmly in the still-wet center of the bull's-eye. Even those who must have bet against him cheered. Nils came to shake his hand, but Mr. Wister stared past him at her.

"What do you think, Mrs. Wilson?" he asked. "Do you need to measure anything?"

She busied herself by beginning to count the money in the pot. "I am entirely comfortable declaring you the winner," she said, avoiding eye contact. "Now let's distribute the winnings and get back to work."

"Keep it for your troubles, Mrs. Wilson," he said, hitching his suspenders back up from where they'd fallen off his shoulders. "I was just playing for the fun of the thing." He reached past the money pile to take a biscuit, and his arm almost brushed against hers. She jumped; no, she had *flinched*. Good Lord, what was the matter with her?

"Now, let's eat!" Mr. Wister declared. "Would be a shame to let all this delicious food go to waste."

Jo gave him what she hoped was a flinty look and retreated to the kitchen to help Ilsa with the serving. Today was going to be a very long day.

Chapter 6

After breakfast, Owen found himself chatting with Nils while Mrs. Wilson fussed over the start of the day's business. About the weather (beautiful!), the fishing (bountiful!), the effects of the hot springs (beneficial!). He found himself speaking in exclamation points: anything to keep the conversation going.

Owen couldn't pinpoint the source of his nervousness. This was, after all, what he'd come to do—to worm his way in and learn the secrets of Wilson's Bathhouse. But what if there was nothing at all untoward going on and he had to return to Vancouver empty-handed? He couldn't bear the condescension of his publisher, who'd grudgingly suggested this assignment only when it was clear that he would never be able to squeeze another novel-writing nickel out of him. *Well, that's that little adventure out of your system,* he would say. *Now what say we buckle on down and write one of those nice wilderness stories? Maybe about the dark continent of Africa this time. Africa's selling like hotcakes these days.* Or what if Mrs. Wilson remained suspicious and kept the less savory aspects of her business hidden away from him? He couldn't afford another slip up, not when those bright grey eyes seemed to track his every step in Fraser Springs.

Finally, Mrs. Wilson announced that she would meet him in the main baths in fifteen minutes. Nils pointed him in the direction of the changing room.

"Have fun," he said, and Owen shook hands before setting his shoulders and addressing himself to the task at hand.

The inner sanctum of the bathhouse resembled a sauna—the air was thick with the same distinctive cedar-scented humidity. Morning light filtered in from narrow vertical windows placed high up on the walls. The mineral springs were hemmed in by smooth planks of cedar, on which men sat in bathing costumes or long johns, their legs dangling into the pool. Some men were submerged up to their necks, likely sitting on platforms installed below the water's surface. Long ago, someone had attempted to give the place Grecian pretensions by installing mosaic tiles on the walls, but the humidity had wreaked havoc on the designs. The figures were blurred away, as if they really had come from an ancient ruin.

The lady attendants were already seated around the perimeter of the room, perched on little wooden stools. Mrs. Wilson herself was standing in front of such a stool, hands clasped behind her back. She nodded curtly for him to sit down. Like the other girls, she wore a white cambric blouse that clung to her arms in the humidity. An opaque white smock concealed the rest of her body, although its nipped-in waist hinted at curves.

The humidity had transformed her curls into an aura around her head, burnished in the angled light of the high windows. A few damp tendrils clung to her neck. Owen felt an urge to sweep the strands away and tuck them back behind her ear. What would happen when all that white fabric got wet? Giving himself a quick mental shake, he dutifully pushed the thoughts away. Here was a woman selling the virtue of innocent girls, and all he could do was stare at her hair and how her collarbone moved beneath the sheer blouse.

"Have a seat," she said, gesturing to the pool's edge. Owen lowered himself gingerly into the water. The water from the hot springs truly was hot, almost painfully so, and it fizzed strangely against his legs. Its mineral odour was even stronger up close. Mrs. Wilson sat down on the stool behind him and lowered her feet into the water next to him, her knees pressed together demurely to one side of his torso. Even in the warm room, the pressure of her legs against him felt warmer.

But despite the outlines of bare arms under sheer blouses, the scene was incongruously chaste. The girls looked more like nurses than light-skirts. And looking around the pool, it was difficult to feel titillated. This rag-tag assortment of miners and loggers certainly didn't seem like the type you'd want to share a bath with. Even when submerged in water, they looked grimy. Their tanned hides were mottled by coarse hair and scars of various vintages, gnarled blue veins, and folds of skin where the muscle was receding and the flesh hung loose. They sat hunched in the steaming water with their eyes closed, like a bunch of scruffy tomcats warming their fur in the sun.

As if he wasn't warm enough, he felt a hot, damp towel lowering into place around his neck. The dense curtain of steam made him feel as if he were inside a dog's mouth.

"To soothe your shoulder and neck muscles," the low voice behind him explained. "Please relax and let me know if you feel any discomfort."

He tried to make a convincing show of relaxation, but he was quite busy ignoring the sensation of a beautiful woman hovering inches away from his body and, of course, studying the scene for clues. The lady attendants bustled about in near silence, providing tall glasses of cool water beaded with condensation, helping men in and out of the pool, pouring water over their heads. They moved in and out of slices of sunlight left by the narrow windows, the light showing flashes of the outline of their limbs and limning their hair with gold. They did not look like nurses after all. With their white uniforms and clean faces, they looked like girls on their way to their first catechism. Perhaps the facade of purity was all part of the show.

The clients smiled and joked with the girls in a brotherly way. He watched the women's hands, waiting for them to make contact with a thigh, a groin, but they stayed primly above waistlines. The men actually seemed more interested in talking to each other than flirting with the staff. On the far side of the pool, a man who was missing the three outermost fingers of his left hand was holding court.

"So he's fresh out of school, this fella, probably never even seen a rock that wasn't in a test tube. Greener than grass. So I says to Slim, let's have a bit of fun with 'im." The pale, smooth scar tissue on his hand shone where the light hit it. Only his thumb and pointer finger remained. The rest of his hand looked like it had been rubbed away with an eraser. "So we go into the office and say, 'Hey there, you're the new guy, Jenkins. How's it going?' He's this nervy, twiggy little man. Scrawny little moustache. Couldn't have been more than twenty-two. So Slim says, 'Welcome to the crew. How're you settlin' in?' and so on. And this young fella's just squirming in his starched collar. Probably never been that close to a body doin' honest work for a living—"

"Or smelled one," a growling voice chimed in.

"Three weeks up at camp and we were ripe that day," the man agreed, chuckling. "Well, you can tell he wants to get back to his lists and numbers, but casual as anything, I sidle up to the pot of hydrofluoric they got there to assay the samples, and I lean my hand against it." He splayed his damaged hand against the cedar floor of the bathhouse to demonstrate. "And just as soon as he glances my way, he squawks, 'Watch out!' I yelp, grab my hand, and start waving it around, screaming, 'My fingers, my fingers! They're gone! Oh Lordy! You've dissolved 'em!'" The other men hoot and clap. Even the lady attendants are smiling. The man chuckles at the memory of his own cleverness.

"Should have seen how white he went. Could practically see right through him. Hah! 'Welcome to the neighbourhood,' I says." He rubbed one knuckle, its scar tissue puckering like a poorly mended dress, and turned to Mrs. Wilson. "Miz Wilson, I should be charging you for providing entertainment for these fellas."

She smiled. "I should be kicking you out for disturbing the peace. Not every customer wants to hear your stories. Do you, Mr. Wister?"

"Aww," said the miner. "I'm just providing some local colour for the town folks. Ain't that what he came up from the fancy city for? A little communion with the common man?"

"Now, Ted ..." Mrs. Wilson said, a note of warning in her voice.

"It's fine," Owen said. "You have a real way with words, Mr. Ted." In truth, he was taking mental notes. He couldn't help thinking of how well the man's story would go over with his young audience. You could have a boy of eleven or twelve—orphaned, maybe—who tries to get work at a mining camp and meets all sorts of characters. And there'd be a mining explosion ... the old miner who took him under his wing was missing ... the boy would have to risk danger in the mine ...

"How is that water feeling, Mr. Wister?" Mrs. Wilson asked.

"Oh, yes," he answered absently. "Wonderful."

"Go ahead and submerge yourself to your neck," she said, standing. "We'll start with ten minutes of exposure." Her voice was clinical and precise. Owen slid into the fizzing water. Nils was clearly wrong. The pill bug wasn't the closest thing to the lobster in these parts —he was.

Thus far, the main baths were a disappointment. He had been sweating like a sinner in church for more than twenty minutes, and he hadn't seen even a hint of scandal. Maybe the real action took place in the private treatment rooms. Or maybe it only happened on certain days. Or between the hours of two and five, like afternoon tea.

Still, the room lacked that tang of physical electricity, that expectant atmosphere that promised something more was about to be revealed. A short time later, Mrs. Wilson returned with a water glass. He hauled himself back onto his bench and drank, enjoying the sensation of the cold water tracing a path down his throat and into his stomach. She pressed her hand to his neck. Her palm was cool and dry, and the unexpected touch made him startle.

"You're getting a bit overheated," she said. When she removed her hand, he could still feel its imprint dissolving into his hot skin. "It's common for first-time clients unless they come from a hot, humid climate. Drink more water, and I'll get you a cool towel."

Owen took another sip of the water and leaned back against the wooden sides of the pool, enjoying the cadence of the men's banter and the fizz of the water against his limbs. The springs were good for relaxation, no doubt. They just didn't seem to be good for his budding journalistic career.

Mrs. Wilson returned with an icy towel that she draped over his head and down his shoulders. The chilly water streamed down his back before mixing with the spring water. "This will help you handle the heat more readily," she explained. She was beginning to perspire, he noticed. Her cheeks were flushed and her forehead damp. The gauzy blouse clung to her arms. Through the fabric, he could just make out the blurry outline of freckles.

"Thank you," he said, trying to give the impression that he was entirely accustomed to being waited on hand and foot. All the bankers he had known cultivated an atmosphere of boredom intended to make you feel insignificant. If she was going to pretend that this was some sort of quasi-medical treatment, then he could pretend, too. He was Mr. Ross Wister of the Toronto Wisters. A trader of stocks, and bonds, and whatever other imaginary nonsense wealthy men bought and sold.

"I'll let you soak for a few minutes longer," she said. "Call if you need anything."

When she left once more, Owen slid closer to the knot of regulars. It was hard to initiate manly contact with a damp towel draped over your head like some kind of nun's habit, but he had wasted enough time sitting quietly. He was, after all, here to work.

"The girls here certainly are pretty, eh?" he said, giving Ted a conspiratorial wink.

Ted nodded. "Yup."

"Yep," agreed another man.

"Sure wouldn't mind getting to know some of them," he said. "I don't suppose you'd know how to arrange that ..."

Ted's shoulders visibly tensed. The other patrons stopped their own conversations to stare at him. "Mister, I think the heat has gone to your head," he said. "Better get yourself a few more cold towels." With that, he stood up. Water sluiced down his wiry body as he grabbed a towel and limped off.

Just then, Mrs. Wilson returned. "Let's get you out of the water," she said. "Towel dry, get changed, and when you're ready, meet me in room six." The men remained aggressively silent, and Owen took the well-timed opportunity to retreat.

Chapter 7

As she changed into a fresh smock, Jo wondered if she had been mistaken about her newest client. He seemed bored by the attendants, bored by the treatments ... and by her. She wasn't sure which Mr. Wister was more unsettling: the one skulking around her windows in the dark of night or the one working so hard to ignore her. Maybe he *was* with the Temperance Society. Did prohibitionists have covert agents? Or perhaps he was simply annoyed with her over the knife-throwing incident this morning. He had seemed in such good spirits then ...

She studied herself in the warped glass of the vanity mirror. The humidity had frizzed and tangled her curls so that her hair looked like a bird's nest. She brushed it out and began to pin it back until there was more metal in her hair than there was in the Yankee Girl Mine. On a whim, she added a tortoiseshell comb that Albert had given her as a wedding gift. He had bought it in Vancouver and had worried that she might find the style old-fashioned. A fifty-year-old man living in the middle of nowhere did not have an eye for ladies' finery, he had nervously explained, but the salesgirl had assured him that it was the very best quality. And he thought it would accentuate the lovely color of her hair, if he might be so forward in saying so.

Recalling Albert's boyish stammering made her feel a pang of bittersweet affection for him. Not the passionate grief of lost love, certainly, but she had been fond of Albert and his big heart. He was such a sincere, good man, and for a year she'd felt secure in the life they had made together. She tried to remember the kind crinkle around his eyes when he smiled.

Best to focus on the task at hand. Albert would be pleased about what she had done with the place. He might not have approved of the lady attendants, no matter how chaste they might be, but he had always told her that even the best establishments ran on compromises. She turned her head in the mirror, admiring the seams of amber and gold that wove through the comb. It wasn't vanity, of course; Mr. Wister needed to stop seeing her as a young woman with tumble-down hair who let him chuck knives in the dining room, and start seeing her as a respectable, prosperous business owner.

She straightened her shoulders. There, that was better: hair in place, clothing starched and crisp, a facade to fortify her when she felt her confidence slipping. If Mr. Wister really was working for the Society Ladies, she would show him that Wilson's offered service superior to all the other bathhouses put together, and she didn't have to break any laws to do it. Let him take that message back to Mrs. McSheen.

When she entered the treatment room, Mr. Wister was standing shirtless, looking out the window at the springs. In her four years at Wilson's Bathhouse, she had seen all manner of backs. The soft swaybacks of men who had dined on goose and jellied eel their whole lives. The hard, wiry backs of working men who seemed to have their life stories scarred into their skin. Mr. Wister's back certainly didn't belong in a leather chair, making deals over claret and meat pies. He was lean and slightly tanned, broad shoulders tapering down to a trim waist. Muscular, but not in the hard-bitten, ropy manner of someone who made their living through hard labour. Where *had* he come from?

"It's quite a view, isn't it?" she said.

He startled and half turned towards her. "Oh," he said. "Yes." Good Lord, the man's front was just as fine as his back. Jo squashed the thought before it could make its way to her face. She saw shirtless men every day, and there was absolutely no reason to come over missish about this one. He was another customer, the first of a dozen she needed to tend to today.

"I'm sorry if I was rude this morning," she said abruptly. "It's just that you caught me off guard. I didn't expect you to come to breakfast after last night."

Mr. Wister reddened faintly. "Ah, well. I'm sure I'm the one who should apologize. I got all turned around. I'm sorry that I startled you."

Jo smiled brightly. "Well, now that we admit we both behaved badly, let's have a fresh start, shall we?" She extended her hand, and after a moment of hesitation, he took it. Something about the firm grip of his warm palm, or maybe the way he looked her straight in the eye as he shook on their truce, made the hair on the back of her neck rise.

She retreated into formality. "Hello, sir. I am Josephine Wilson, proprietress of this establishment."

He sketched a brief, equally formal bow, amusement in his blue eyes. "And a good day to you as well, ma'am. I am Ross Wister, lowly customer."

"A pleasure to make your acquaintance," she said. "Now, lie down on your stomach, and we'll begin to fix what ails you."

He did as he was told, easing himself onto the tin-topped treatment table and shifting about to settle his weight. Ilsa bustled in with a damp towel and a bowl of mint-scented oil, filling the room with the sharp green odour. Jo nodded her thanks, but Ilsa paused to shoot an exaggeratedly admiring glance at Mr. Wister's back stretched out in front of her. Jo rolled her eyes and silently jerked her head towards the door. Ilsa left, grinning.

Time to get to work. She laid the towel across that distracting back and set the bowl down on the little table by the window. "We'll begin with massage. I will apply warm oil to loosen your muscles and mint to ease any tension," she explained. He made a noise that sounded like assent.

Jo poured a palmful of the liquid and rubbed her hands to coat them. In truth, her massage "technique" was cobbled together from bits and pieces she'd learned from Albert and bathhouse attendants past and present, plus a few flourishes thrown in from magazine illustrations of Turkish bathhouses. Experience, however, had refined the motions into a smooth, practiced routine.

She drizzled more salve into the hollow of his lower back, then used her palms to sweep it upwards in half-circles towards his shoulder blades. Mr. Wister tensed, then gradually relaxed into the rhythm of her hands. She moved across his skin's topography in widening arcs, noting the tension eddying in the muscles, the strange pockets where the body held pain. It was odd, she'd always thought, how easy it was to track where a person hurt.

She felt a small, particularly knotted, tight node of muscle at the base of his skull, where the hair was shaved close. The hairs rose almost imperceptibly as she brushed her fingers over the spot. She did it again, just to feel the shush of hairs yielding to her sensitive fingertips. Mr. Wister's back rose and fell with his deepening breathing. She was close enough to him to detect his shaving soap and sweat beneath the pungency of the salve. She leaned forward and pressed her thumbs, hard, into the knotted muscle.

"Umph," was all Mr. Wister said, and she briefly thought he was falling asleep. But no, his body didn't lie. She could feel it when men settled into sleep on her table. Their muscles slackened, their arms hung lower. But Mr. Wister was alert, his pulse rapid beneath her fingertips. Perhaps too rapid. Well, at least he was paying attention.

"I want you to take a deep breath," she said, surprised at the low crackle in her voice. "It's important to remove the source of the tension."

She leaned forward and pressed her thumb into the knot. "Breathe," she reminded quietly, close against his ear. "Just keep breathing and let me do all the work."

When she released the knot, he sighed. His shoulders sank. She skimmed her fingernails slowly, lightly down along his spine. Now, why had she done that? The movement was not a part of her routine. This man's smooth, lean back was not particularly special, after all, even if it did exhibit some distracting contradictions.

As she leaned forward to dig her palm into another knot, a rebellious lock of hair came loose and brushed across the small of his back, as if painting it. Mr. Wister shuddered like a horse twitching off a fly. Though she knew hair had no feeling, the gesture made her scalp tickle. She was suddenly aware of the tortoiseshell comb digging into her temple.

"Sorry," she murmured and tucked the strand back into place.

He didn't acknowledge her apology. She drizzled another thin line of green-tinted oil between his shoulders and moved her palms in small circles, kneading the warm salve into his skin, willing it into his muscles where it would melt away the hard little knots. All the nerves in her hands felt charged, probably tingling from the mint. She tried to focus, to enter that pleasant state in which her own thoughts and worries disappeared into the single-mindedness of work, but for the next quarter hour, her concentration eluded her. The strange sensation in her hands and her loosening hair were distracting. The air in the room felt increasingly thick, as if the humidity of the bathhouse had permeated the door.

"I think," she said, finally, "that should have you taken care of for today. Are you still comfortable?" Mr. Wister made a vague assenting noise deep in his throat. "Excellent. I'll rinse you down, and you can be on your way." She turned to the basin of cold water by the window and proceeded as efficiently as she could. Final ablutions complete, she turned to the window once again and spent more time than was perhaps strictly necessary to soap and scrub her hands. Mr. Wister rose, donned his shirt and tie, and exited the room without a word.

After he left, Jo daubed water on her face and the back of her neck. Even after the scrubbing, her palms still buzzed with the mint and friction of the massage. She splashed more water on her face, trying to clear her blurry thoughts by concentrating on the view from the window. Summer was beginning in earnest, and soon Fraser Springs would be thick with mosquitos and a mineral-laden fog of humidity. In the summer, the mountains that loomed over the town made her feel as if she were stuck in an enormous soup tureen.

Ilsa bustled in to collect the towels and bowls for cleaning. "Well, then. Does he feel as good as he looks?" she teased.

Jo shot her what she hoped was a bland, utterly unruffled glare. "Ilsa, can you air out this room? It is impossibly stifling. I suspect the summer heat will be settling on us sooner than expected."

Isla did not even bother to hide her grin. "Of course. We will talk about the weather. Whatever you say, Miz Jo."

Jo's retort, however, was cut short by the sudden sound of breaking glass. Without thinking, both women ran down to the front parlour. The floor was strewn with shards of clear and blue glass, smashed into an almost lovely wave on the floor. Broken window glass, broken bottles, and in the center of the glittering mess sat a brick wrapped in paper like a gift. It even had a ribbon tied around it.

"Be careful." Ilsa touched Jo's shoulder. "They could still be here."

She brushed off the hand. "Those cowards couldn't look me in the eye, let alone hurt us." She bent down to pick up the brick when Nils came running through the front door.

"What happened?" he asked, looking between the two women. Jo silently gestured to the brick, and Nils went very still. Then he nodded and turned back towards the door. "I'll be right back."

"Nils, don't." The man's knuckles clenched at his sides, but he stopped where he was. "All you'll do is earn yourself a few nights in the lock-up and your name in the paper. 'Bathhouse Thug Commits Unprovoked Assault on Upstanding Citizens.'"

Nils's jaw jutted forward. "But they'll have time to think twice about terrorizing women while they're nursing their broken faces."

Jo approached him, skirting the broken glass as best she could, and laid her hand on his shoulder. "Even if you caught them, you know it will only make things worse. We need you here, Nils. We can't afford to have you locked up."

He gave a long, frustrated sigh. "I can't just stand by."

"Then help us clean up. And come with us to the meeting. Then you can stare these cowards straight in the eye and call them out in front of everyone."

As she spoke, Jo untied the ribbon from around the brick, brushed the crumbs of glass off the paper, and read:

"For the lips of a strange woman drop as a honeycomb, and her mouth is smoother than oil: But her end is bitter as wormwood, sharp as a two-edged sword. Her feet go down to death; her steps take hold on hell. Proverbs 5:3-5."

She refolded the letter neatly. "Hypocrites. Blasphemous, cowardly hypocrites." She tucked it into her smock's pocket.

Another love letter for her collection.

Really, though, what she had told Nils was nothing but the truth. Right now, anger was less helpful than industry.

"The men will be here for supper soon," she announced as much to herself as to her employees. No, to her friends. "We need to get this mess sorted."

Ilsa nodded and collected brooms for them from the hall closet. Jo began to sweep, but almost immediately something caught her eye among the splintered window glass. She bent down and picked up a shard with the letters W I L written in gold paint. Wilson's. If Albert were still alive, there'd be no discontent in the town at all. He'd have soothed it away in an afternoon. *"Oh, Mrs. McSheen, we all know it's the Lord's work to reform fallen women by setting them to honest, meaningful labour. Now, tell me how young Emma is coming along with her piano lessons—"* He'd lead her away for a cup of tea, and before long, she'd be trumpeting that Wilson's Bathhouse was a righteous establishment fulfilling a higher purpose. Jo sighed. Maybe she had brought this on herself. She was too inflexible, unable to talk sweet.

The glass made a rasping, tinkling sound as she and Ilsa swept the pieces across the floor and into piles. Nils returned with wood to board up the window. As the daylight gradually dimmed and then disappeared from the parlour, Jo had the brief, panicked sensation of being buried alive. Oh, she would miss the light the window brought in. No one in town made glass panes of that size. A new window would have to be shipped up from Vancouver. How would she even begin to find the money?

In the middle of her sweeping, Ilsa looked up and stared at the space where the window had been.

"What's wrong?" Jo asked.

"Do you think Mr. Wister had anything to do with this? He just left from his treatment, and all of a sudden there's a brick through our window."

"Aww, he's a good sort," Nils said.

Jo paused. His racing pulse, the cords of tension in his neck and shoulders. All that time she was massaging him, was he reciting Bible passages to himself and imagining her face when she saw his handiwork? "I ... I don't think so. No. The handwriting matches the other notes, so unless he's been here for months ..."

"Or unless he's working with someone," Ilsa said.

"Why bother sending in a spy if he already had his mind made up enough to smash my window in broad daylight? And he wasn't gone five minutes before this happened. Why throw the brick right after he left if he wanted to avoid suspicion?"

Jo had never seen Ilsa angry before. Now, however, a flush spread across her cheeks and throat, and her wide blue eyes narrowed. "I don't know why you're defending him. You said yourself he's hiding something. We caught him prowling around our house last night!"

"You didn't tell me that," said Nils, bristling.

"Do I think he's hiding something? Yes. Do I think he spent all day here, found absolutely nothing, and then wrote a Bible verse on a brick he just happened to have on his person so he could throw it through the front window? No. We need to be calm and rational about this."

"I don't think he means to harm anyone," Nils said after a silence. "But you do need to be careful."

Ilsa swept the floor with such force that the broom looked like it was about to snap, avoiding everyone's gaze. "

Jo wanted to tell her that it would be all right. They'd replace the glass. They'd get through the season. But the words felt like dust in her throat when she tried to speak them. Instead, she doubled her cleaning efforts. Was Ross Wister behind all this? Could she really be trying to hurt her?

Chapter 8

Owen didn't clearly remember his walk back to the St. Alice. His brain was still buzzing loudly enough that when he entered the bright, echoing hotel he wouldn't have noticed if it had contained a brass band at full volume. He asked for his key at the desk and crossed the gleaming lobby. The smell of mint and talc clung to him, the odors indelibly linked to the friction of soft palms sliding against his naked back, his shoulders, his neck. The sluicings of cold water he had been subjected to afterwards had restored him to enough decency to leave the room with his dignity intact, but the effect seemed to be short-lived.

He marched up the stairs to his room, taking them two at a time. He tried to be fascinated by the carpet pattern. The colour of the wallpaper. It was ridiculous wallpaper. She was a ridiculous, intolerable woman. At last, he was through the door to his room. He locked it behind him and leaned his forehead against the cool, solid wood. He could still smell mint. With a groan, he released the door handle and stripped off his strangling tie and his coat. He walked across the room to the washstand, where the smooth heft of the porcelain pitcher reminded him impossibly of her cool hands.

It was no good. No matter how fervently he instructed his thoughts to turn their course, he could only recall the images that had flooded his imagination in that claustrophobic little room. Her hair escaping its pins, curling down the back of her neck. Her lips, pale pink and soft, parted ever so slightly as she leaned over him. The sweet, curving flare of her hips as she swiveled and bent, calling out for him to place his hands there and pull her to him.

He was fully hard now, straining painfully against the restriction of his trousers. The curtains were drawn. There was no one to see him. And there was no use at all pretending that he had the willpower to keep from addressing this madness directly.

With a deep sigh, he set down the pitcher. He retrieved his handkerchief, unbuttoned his trousers, and finally let himself visualize the things he wanted to do to Josephine Wilson in that quiet, private room. No reason to be gentle. He imagined turning her around and bending her over that cold, tin tabletop. She'd gasp as he rucked up her petticoat and pushed her thighs apart. Her hips would press against his groin as he pushed into her. He settled into the familiar rhythm, and everything fell away except the illusory sensations of her body tensing and arching beneath him.

He let his release wash over him. When, after what felt like years, it was over, he slumped weakly against the footboard, his head hanging, fingers of his right hand still curled loosely around his lightly pulsing cock. His breath came in shallow gasps. He refused to feel ashamed. There was nothing wrong with this, not after the torture he'd been through this afternoon. Nothing at all.

And he was going back for more tomorrow. Jesus Christ. He freed himself from the rest of his clothing and collapsed onto the bed.

• • •

That night, Jo brought out the other love letters the town had sent her. She had been storing them in a chocolate box in her desk, all the anonymous notes, Bible verses, letters to the editor signed "A Concerned Citizen." If nothing else, the Society Ladies had excellent penmanship. Sometimes she marveled at what ugly words could be written in such a beautiful script.

Jo spread the letters on her bed and let her eyes wander between them until the words blurred together like voices in some angry, silent choir. She knew what her father would say. *"Don't wrestle with a pig, sweetheart. You'll just get dirty, and the pig will enjoy it."* But how else could she defend herself? It wasn't easy to turn the other cheek when she was sweeping up broken glass.

She smoothed the most recent letter. What advice would her father or Albert give? She could not conjure their voices. If the two men were still alive, she wouldn't be in this situation. Had her father been cured, they'd likely be living in Vancouver or Victoria. Maybe she'd be married. Maybe she'd be working as a pattern maker. After so long in the country, the only noise of civilization she could still imagine was a train whistle. If Albert hadn't taken a heart attack, the townspeople would have been forced to at least tolerate her.

The only place she truly felt safe was in the bathhouse. Wilson's had problems, but they were problems with clear solutions. If fresh meat was scarce, she stretched what she had into a stew and served it to hungry customers along with loaves of fresh bread. If the roof leaked, she patched it. She trusted her girls and Nils, and they trusted her. Within the walls of the bathhouse, she was in control.

But the broken window was a problem she didn't know how to solve. She didn't know where to get the money for more glass, and even if she came up with the money, there would be another brick, another letter. Leaving was out of the question. Where else would she go? And what would happen to the girls if she left? Try as she might, she couldn't see herself anywhere but where she was: alone, with the fury of Fraser Springs directed against her. She would have to come up with her own solution.

Chapter 9

Owen woke with a start the next morning. Usually, nothing stood between him and supper, especially not sleep. Sleep was such a waste of time. All the men he knew and admired slept no more than six hours a night. Still, aside from a growling stomach, his mood had improved considerably. Not many people got paid to enjoy the professional ministrations of a beautiful woman, let alone with the chance to make a real difference in the world while doing so. He whistled tunelessly as he attended to his morning toiletries. Ahead of him lay a hearty breakfast, a soak in a steam bath, and ... he refused to let his mind wander. Regardless, it was shaping up to be an excellent day.

"Sir, a moment of your time," a woman's voice piped behind his shoulder just as he placed his hand on the lobby door handle.

Owen turned, startled. Before him stood a woman supplied with an armful of leaflets and a sour expression. She was one of those people born perpetually looking fifty, even though he guessed by the small child whose hand she was holding that she was no more than thirty. A heavy scent of rosewater filled a three-foot radius around her.

"Forgive me, I don't believe we've been formally introduced," she said, inclining her head slightly in a careful nod; her heavily plumed hat must have weighed at least ten pounds. "I am Mrs. McSheen. This is my daughter Emma."

"Ross Wister," he said, "A pleasure to make your acquaintance. And you, too, Miss Emma." Both McSheens smiled, though the elder fought hard to retain her dour expression. "It's a lovely town you have here."

"Yes. That is precisely what I wished to speak with you about." She offered him a leaflet. *Deliver Fraser Springs from the Jaws of Sin!* its headline read. "Fraser Springs *is* a lovely town, but it deeply saddens me to tell you that some of the local establishments are ... less than savory. I am the president and co-founder of the Society for the Advancement of Moral Temperance. Which is why it falls to me to caution you." She lowered her voice. "I've been informed by concerned parties that you have patronized Wilson's Bathhouse. In ignorance, surely."

"I was told it was the best." He shouldn't be surprised that his comings and goings were common knowledge in this small town.

"You were, unfortunately, very badly misinformed," she said, her disapproval barely hidden behind her sweet tone. "I'm not sure if you noticed—I'm confident you would not intentionally venture into such a place—but Wilson's Bathhouse is ..." she put her hands over her daughter's ears, "a house of *ill repute.*" Her voice was a melodramatic hiss now.

Owen was caught between the pleasure of finally having his suspicions confirmed and the sinking feeling that he might have found the source of the rumours that had brought him to Fraser Springs. "I can assure you, ma'am, I haven't seen anything of that sort going on," he said. "But I appreciate your concern."

She leaned towards him; the combination of his empty stomach and her rosewater was nauseating. "I would simply hate for your time here to be tainted by an error in judgment," she said. "You probably confused the St. Alice with Wilson's. Any good Christian would understand. This leaflet contains all the information you need to set you right." She thrust one of her papers at him; he took it reflexively. "We're holding a meeting tomorrow, and it would be of great help to our cause if you could testify on what you saw in that pit of vipers."

"Ma'am, I haven't—"

"It's one thing for those miners and loggers to succumb to sin. They're half-wild. You can't expect anything else from that sort. But we must stop the spread of contagion before it reaches the virtuous." She lowered her voice and jabbed at line in the leaflet. "See here? I explain right here that when a foot is infected, the doctor must amputate to save the patient. If we think of the town as a body, then it's clear that certain parts of Fraser Springs have become gangrenous. We must cut them off at the source and allow Christ to cauterize the wound."

Good Lord. Amputations? Gangrene? What were these demented people planning?

"Your leaflet contains lies and slander." A woman's voice rang down the boardwalk as the pale young lady from the bathhouse, currently carrying a string sack of potatoes in her clenched fists, muscled her way between Mrs. McSheen and him. Mrs. McSheen positively recoiled. "If you were the Christians you claim to be, you wouldn't be trying to ruin the livelihoods of innocent people. Not to mention damaging their property! What happened to 'let he without sin cast the first stone'?"

Mrs. McSheen looked as if she would desperately like to swoon for dramatic effect, but she settled for placing her palm on her chest and swaying slightly. "I'm sure I don't know what you're talking about," she snapped. "We are simply trying to rid this town of … of impure influences." She recovered herself long enough to produce a formidable glare. "Like yourself, Ilsa Pedersen." The little girl stared at the young lady more in fascination than in fear.

Ilsa ignored Mrs. McSheen to finally acknowledge Owen's presence. "And you! I knew you were in it like thieves with this lot. Jo and Nils may defend you because you can throw some silly knife into a stump, but I see your stripes."

Mrs. McSheen grasped at her daughter's hand and began to pull her past Ilsa in the direction of the boardwalk, startling the child. "I don't have to stand here and listen to you make wild accusations." She brandished her leaflets in the bathhouse girl's direction, as if trying to ward off evil spirits. "The devil is here, sir, right here in our town. And we won't stop until we cast him out."

With that, she tramped down the boardwalk toward the safety of the other Society Ladies, who had been pointedly pretending not to listen to the entire conversation. The blond young woman spun on her heel and marched away in the opposite direction, leaving Owen standing alone in front of the hotel steps. There was nothing quite like the machinations of a league of women to set a man on his ear.

He looked around: faces peeped out of the hotel windows, admiring the lake with a quite singular focus. Another cluster of onlookers gazed from the bank's steps, seeming unusually interested in the clouds over the trees. An entire town of studious nature lovers. Whatever was going on at Wilson's Bathhouse, it was a miracle that Jo was able to hide it.

When he arrived, the front window was boarded up. A hand-lettered sign propped in the windowsill read *We Are Open*. He passed through into the front room and saw the blond young lady, sans potatoes, carrying an armload of towels through a doorway to his right.

"Excuse me, miss? What happened here?" he asked.

"No, no, no," she said. "I told you. I see through all of your stripes!" Still holding the towels, she made a dismissive gesture. "Acting like a good man, and then you turn around and cost us hundreds! And at the start of the season!" Even in the gloom of the boarded-up bathhouse, he could see the anger in her eyes. She strode off towards the changing room.

Owen followed her. "I beg your pardon! Are you accusing *me* of breaking your window?"

"I'm sure there are any number of things I could accuse you of doing, mister." Her voice had risen enough that the exchange might attract the attention of the men in the dining room. Or worse, Mrs. Wilson.

"Perhaps we can discuss this in private?" he asked in his most reasonable tone of voice.

Her blue eyes narrowed. "Like you were discussing with Mrs. McSheen? No. I'm not going anywhere with you. I almost wish you'd been a pervert. You're worse."

Did she know the real reason for his trip? How could she have possibly found out? "Would you care to be more specific, miss?" he asked.

The woman was so pale that her eyebrows were almost invisible, but there was no mistaking her baleful expression. "You leave after your treatment. Not five minutes later a brick comes crashing through our window. Now you're having a rat's chat with Mrs. McSheen. You come in, pretend to be a customer, throw the money around, make friends, and all the while you're trying to betray us."

Owen felt a pang in his gut that didn't come from hunger. She was right in the wrong way. He had lied, but he'd done it for a good reason. "You said someone threw a *brick* through that window? Intentionally?"

"Yes," Ilsa said. "It shattered all the pretty bottles and the whole Wilson's sign. Another piece of Scripture wrapped on a brick and delivered by the good Christians of Fraser Springs."

"Was anyone hurt?"

"No, but we can't afford to send away for new glass all the way from Vancouver. And how are we supposed to attract customers with a boarded-up front, right at the beginning of the season?" She suddenly looked as if she might cry.

"That's terrible," he said. "I can assure you that it wasn't my doing. I don't mean you any harm." Except that he did. The article that could make his career would ruin Mrs. Wilson's, land her in jail even, but only if she were guilty. So far, the evidence against her was just hearsay and rumour, and it was hard to side with people who seemed to express their beliefs by way of property damage.

"It was cruel," she said.

"It was. It was a cowardly act, but I didn't do it."

Ilsa stared straight at him. She was calm now, straight-backed and clear-eyed. She did not seem like a woman with anything to hide. "I have work to attend to, Mr. Wister. Excuse me."

With that, she brushed past him and disappeared down a hallway. Owen thought of the fancy suit that hung from the hook on the bathroom door. The gold watch was cool in his pocket. Silly theatrics, all of it. He was better at writing stories than acting them out.

All this distance, all this time and money, and it seemed that his big scoop was nothing more than the nasty gossip of bored church ladies. Some journalist he was, ready to destroy the reputation of a woman just trying to get by after the death of her husband. The clumsy sneaking around, the false identity: it suddenly seemed not merely awkward but utterly, comically inept, too. He was going to return to Vancouver a fool. Worse: a failure. His appetite suddenly gone, he thought about going back to bed and sleeping off his embarrassment and disappointment until he could slink home on tomorrow morning's boat. But no. He had come all this way and was not about to leave empty-handed. He could be Ross Wister for another few days if it meant getting something honest into print.

Chapter 10

Jo woke up angry at herself, angry at the town, and angry at Ross Wister. She'd dreamed about him again. What had gotten into her? Her bathhouse was under attack and she was distracted by schoolgirl dreams. Despite his charm, the man was nothing more than a stranger with questionable intentions, who might well be conspiring with the Society Ladies to run her out of town.

Embarrassing as it might be to admit, the explanation for his presence in her dreams was likely simple enough. She was ... drawn to him, physically. He was undeniably handsome, and he had such a lovely, open smile. It had been so long since a man had smiled at her the way he had during that knife-throwing incident yesterday morning. For all the gossip about the temptation and seduction to be found at Wilson's, she'd lived like the abbess of a nunnery since Albert's death. It was gratifying to be flirted with, end of story. A little vanity: that was all there was to whatever passing interest she might have in Mr. Ross Wister.

Still, a nagging inner voice reminded her as climbed out of bed, she had been wrong about men before. She'd thought Albert was a decent man with whom she could build a secure life. Though she'd been right about the first part, she could not have been more wrong about the second. Clearly, her judgment could not be trusted.

She finished dressing and headed downstairs to help the girls with breakfast but found that, once again, she had badly overslept and the meal was set. The regular patrons sat shoveling food in silence. Mr. Wister and Nils sat together, though Mr. Wister did not seem to be paying attention to anything Nils said or to her entrance. He stared into his coffee mug, lost in his own thoughts.

The boarded-up window gave the room the gloomy hush of pre-dawn. Ilsa, who was filling coffee cups, avoided her gaze and wasn't joking with the patrons as she normally would. Likely embarrassed by her outburst last night. But was Jo the one who should be embarrassed? Was she allowing Ross Wister to spy on her in exchange for a few charming smiles and winks? She tried to read his expression but kept recalling how he looked in the lamplight, his eyes studying her so intently.

"Ilsa, can you bring the oil lamps for the tables? No one can see their food."

Ilsa set down the coffee carafe. "Right away, ma'am." Gone was the easy smile, the chirpy "Yes, Miz Jo."

The possible reasons for Ross Wister's presence nagged at Jo as she managed the toast and coffee. They nagged at her as she attended to him, still silent and distracted, in the bathhouse. The brick incident had cast a pall over the main soaking room. Even the usually gregarious miners sat staring forward or towards the high, vertical windows. Everyone seemed lost in thought.

It wasn't until the massage treatments that she relaxed into the rhythm of the day. Ross Wister was already undressed to the waist and lying facedown on the treatment table when she entered. He looked up and nodded a greeting. Like Ilsa, he avoided eye contact.

"How are you today?" she asked as she laid out the towels, cringing at the chill in her voice. Dammit if she didn't keep seeing him as in the dream: touching her face, staring into her eyes. The outline of his muscles tapered down towards the two divots on his lower back, and his skin was faintly sheened with sweat already. She tried to force the professionalism back into her voice. What kind of proprietress was she?

Soon, Ilsa came in with fresh supplies. When Mr. Wister saw her, his gaze quickly flicked elsewhere and his shoulders rose with tension. Was there something between them? She ruthlessly suppressed the pang of—jealousy? No, merely annoyance. Maybe this mystery was the oldest, most predictable secret in the book: he was attracted to buxom nineteen-year-olds.

"Thank you," Jo said. "That should be everything for now."

Ilsa nodded and left the room hastily. Mr. Wister seemed to relax.

The moment the warm oil made contact with her palms, Jo relaxed as well. Her hands kneaded and smoothed taut muscle, moving with the mindless confidence of long practice. They found the hidden knots of tension under the skin and traced their sources across his back. She loved the strength of her hands, the feeling of satisfaction she got when a knot released and a man's pain fell away. She might not be able to predict the bricks through her window or the future of Wilson's Bathhouse, but in this room, at this moment, she was in complete control.

"Am I allowed to converse with you during this, or is it customary to keep mum and drift off to sleep?" he suddenly asked.

She did not break the rhythm of her motions. "Most do. Keep quiet, that is. Others, though ... I think some men pay for someone to talk to, more than anything."

"They get lonely." He didn't phrase it as a question.

She worked her way towards his lower back. "I suppose so. And then some people are just natural talkers, and there are more of them than there are natural listeners. The talkers get a captive audience this way."

"And are you a natural listener?" he asked, almost playfully.

She poured more oil onto her hands. Truly, the man held tension everywhere. "I take it you're a talker, then. What's on your mind, sir?"

"Touché, madam." She felt as well as heard his smile. Funny how when someone smiled you could feel it ripple throughout their muscles. "I'm afraid that my mind is a perfect and uninterrupted expanse of emptiness."

"Then what could possibly be causing these headaches of yours, I wonder?"

She'd reached the base of his spine and was pressing her thumb into the hollows there.

He sighed, and the lightness was suddenly gone from their conversation. "To be honest, headaches don't trouble me overmuch. And I don't think my nerves are all that unsound. I'm not an invalid."

She wasn't sure how to respond to this admission, and the silence stretched.

"I'm just not ... all that happy, really. In my work, that is."

Another long pause. Jo focused on making perfectly circular motions with her fingertips. The man's unhappiness was no concern of hers. "It was supposed to be a temporary thing, you know. Just something to do until I got my feet under me. I have a talent for it, and it seemed like the obvious thing to make a little money. And it was fun, at first. The thrill of victory, you know."

"Mmm," Jo made a vaguely encouraging noise as she worked down towards his shoulders.

"And then I looked up, and years have gone by, and I'm still going over the same ground, and the joy's just completely gone from it. I'm repeating the motions, and one day I realized that I'm practically doing them in my sleep. I've been at it almost ten years, and I don't have one thing to show for it that I can feel really proud of."

"I'm sure that's not true," she murmured. Why was she encouraging him? This wasn't the kind of confession she needed from him.

He snorted. "All I've thought about for months now is taking every scrap of paper I've ever scribbled on and burning it to ash." Jo's hands stilled, although he didn't seem to register the loss of soothing motion. "I'm a damned ungrateful bastard, forgive the language, and I know it. I know there's a raft of men—probably women too—who'd give their eyeteeth for what I've got. I've got a soft life, and that's the truth. A safe, sheltered, soft little life."

He practically spat the words out, and his own vehemence startled him back into self-awareness. All of her work had come undone. His back was taut. "I'm sorry," he said into the stillness. "I suppose I'm a talker after all."

"It's no trouble," she said a little too lightly and busied her hands again with renewed briskness.

They continued in silence.

Finally, quietly, she spoke. "It's not that unusual, if it helps any."

"Beg pardon?"

"The way you feel. That you're just marking the time without ever going anywhere. That you haven't made the right choices."

"Are you speaking from personal experience, Mrs. Wilson?" In any other room, the question might have been a flirtation. Now, however, he sounded utterly in earnest, as if the answer meant a great deal to him.

"We all make mistakes, Mr. Wister," she replied, slowly. "We make the best choices we can, in the moment, and try to live with them afterwards. And I'm sure we make mistakes in that as well." Even to her own ears, she sounded so tired as she made this pronouncement, more deeply weary than a woman still in her twenties should be.

She turned away and began rattling shut little pots and tins, opening drawers to retrieve clean cloths, and shuffling the soiled ones into a little hamper at one side of the room. Owen seemed to recognize her sudden burst of industry as channeled discomfort and took his cue. He sat up, reaching for his shirt.

At the sound, Jo turned her head slightly. "Mr. Wister, may I ask you a question? While we're being honest."

He froze. "Of course, Mrs. Wilson."

"If you're not an invalid, why are you here?"

• • •

Everything depended on how he answered her, and yet he shrank from the lies that sprang immediately to mind. He took a deep breath. His skin buzzed with the effects of the massage, but his mind was suddenly totally clear. Oh, to hell with it. To hell with the whole pockmarked farce.

"I lied to you when we met. I didn't come here for my health. I came here ... well, on a mission, I suppose."

He couldn't look at her. He didn't want to see the reaction in those pale grey eyes. Jo Wilson was perfectly, breathlessly still. Not a single fold in her skirts shifted.

"You see, I'm a writer. I finally convinced my publisher to give me a shot at journalism ... and he'd heard rumors about this place ...."

He finally summoned the courage to look into her eyes. Her brows were furrowed, her gaze unreadable. "A writer," she echoed, slowly.

"A writer," he confirmed. "I write novels, mostly. Not very good ones. I thought that a bit of muckraking might be the start of something new for me. You know, young girls lured from their homes with promises of honest employment, trapped in a den of iniquity and vice, and all that." The premise seemed patently absurd when spoken aloud in this spartan little room. "I'm sorry. I was misinformed."

She busied her hands by folding a towel and smoothed away whatever expression was on her face. "Ah. Well, then. I hope you've found us thoroughly disappointing, Mr. Wister." Her voice was perfectly controlled. She could have been commenting on the weather.

In for a penny, in for a pound. He'd probably already offended her beyond redemption. "That's another lie, I'm afraid. The name, I mean." He held out his hand. "Owen Sterling. Pleased to make your acquaintance."

Her own hands stayed firmly tucked the towel. "I don't suppose you lobbed a brick through my front window to make your story a little more dramatic, did you, Mr. Whomever?"

He kept his hand stubbornly extended. "Sterling. No, of course not. Complete waste of a good brick, if you ask me."

Damn. He shouldn't have made a joke of that. But before he could apologize, her steely expression had softened. She gingerly reached out her own hand, and he seized it before she could change her mind. Her hands were still slick from the massage oil and warmed from the effort of her work. He felt the calluses on her palms and the pads of her fingers.

The sensation made him suddenly aware that his shirt was unbuttoned and hanging open. He'd been so distracted by his own troubles that he'd completely forgotten about his state of undress. He released her hand as quickly as he'd taken it.

"Will you be leaving us, then?"

"I haven't quite made up my mind as to that," he responded, buttoning his shirt in what was, hopefully, an entirely unselfconscious way. The salve from her hands lingered on his as he struggled with the buttons. "I'll readily admit that this has been a less than ideal trip in terms of exposing vice, but I'm not in a burning rush to get back to Vancouver. I believe I'm paid up through the week here?"

"Through Monday next, actually."

"How extravagant of me."

She nodded, no doubt confirming his lack of thrift. "Am I to understand that you won't be so free with your pocketbook now that you're no longer a financial gentleman?"

"I beg your pardon." He might not be a banker, but he wasn't a charity case either. "How do you know I'm not a celebrated and wealthy author?"

"Because you said you weren't very good. And because if you were celebrated and wealthy, I would have heard of you, Mr. Sterling." He couldn't quite tell if she was being serious. Her tone was matter-of-fact, but that wry little smile was still haunting the corners of her eyes.

"You wound me, Mrs. Wilson. I'll have you know that my work is extremely popular." *With young boys and your handyman.*

"I suppose it would be, if your usual subject is ... I'm sorry, remind me again what you thought you'd find here? Captive virgins, I believe?" She was teasing him now; he was absolutely sure of it.

"I'm beginning to suspect the establishment is staffed entirely by Amazons," he grumbled.

There, she laughed at that. "That would be a fair sight closer to the truth, I'm afraid." Was this the first time he'd heard her laugh? It was such a bright, happy sound that he was inordinately pleased with himself for having drawn it from her. He smiled back at her.

And suddenly the little smile was gone again, and Mrs. Wilson was all bustle and business. "At any rate, if you prefer to leave early, I'm sure we could refund a portion of your payment. There might be a small delay, expenses being what they are at the moment, but if you'd care to leave your Vancouver address with us, we can forward a cheque ..." Owen levered onto his feet, mystified, as she continued on, something about the postal service and railway timetables.

She was halfway out the door before he could get a word in edgewise. "Mrs. Wilson." She spun to face him, her torrent of managerial chatter cut off mid-sentence. "If it's all the same to you, I'd prefer to stay the duration."

"Oh. Of course. I only thought that since you don't have any ailments that need treating ..."

"This would be a sort of holiday from the strains of being such a celebrated and wealthy author." Her little smile surfaced again, then was gone once more. It suddenly seemed powerfully important that he make Jo Wilson laugh again. "I won't waste any more of your time on curing my nervous conditions, and you needn't bother with posting that refund cheque. I only have one condition. No, two conditions."

She looked wary but nodded for him to continue. "I'd like to at least keep up the appearance of being a client here. Too much explaining, otherwise."

"We could arrange that, certainly," she replied. "And the second condition, Mr. Sterling?"

"It's really more in the nature of a request than a condition. I would appreciate it if we could be more at ease with each other. For a start, you could call me Owen." He held out his hand again.

Regardless of the outcome, the honesty felt good. Maybe he would never be a journalist. Maybe he would be stuck writing children's books forever. But right now, with his hand outstretched towards Jo Wilson, none of that seemed to matter. He would stay, but for purely journalistic reasons. He owed it to himself to see if the rogue brick thrower could be some kind of story. Not front page material, but all journalists had to start somewhere.

Chapter 11

Jo stared at his proffered hand. He looked so earnest and relieved. The confession seemed to have done him more good than even her best massage. Then again, he had also just admitted to targeting her with a campaign of lies and deceit. She kept her own hand firmly on the doorknob.

At her hesitation, he ran his hand through his hair and stepped a little closer. "I know we've made a bad start." He grimaced. "Twice, actually."

"I almost shot you night before last," she reminded him.

"Yes, but you didn't pull the trigger, did you?" he asked cheerfully. "You also haven't told me to leave and never come back. In fact, you've been rather pleasant to me since then."

"Another instance of poor judgment, clearly."

Lord, he had such an easy smile. "Oh, I don't think so." He raised an eyebrow at her. "You're a smart woman. And I think you believe me when I tell you that while I may be a fool, I have only the best intentions."

Jo sighed. That was true. She'd been trying hard to be suspicious of Mr. Wister ... Mr. Sterling ... Owen—whoever he was. But her gut wouldn't stop telling her that there was something decent about the man. It was not clear, however, whether her woman's intuition was confusing goodness of character with firmness of muscles. "As I said before," she said, "you are welcome to stay."

Owen clapped his hands together, as if they'd just decided to host a party. "Then it's settled. Excellent. I'll stay, and we'll be on good terms. Which means I can address you as ...?" The man was impossible. It was like trying to be formal with a Labrador retriever.

"Jo," she said, and she smiled. "But only in private."

"Agreed. Shake on it, Jo?" He was treating her with the same easy openness he'd used with the crowd in her dining room yesterday morning. She wouldn't have been surprised if he'd spat in his open palm before extending it to her. It was improbably charming.

"As you like, Owen." She clasped his hand for the second time that afternoon.

"There," he said quietly. "That's better."

He was staring at her just the way he had in those dreams. Jo flinched and pulled her hand back.

"Oh, are you all right?" He looked genuinely concerned.

"No, it's nothing. It's not—" She could not suppress the dream. What was the matter with her? "It's not—" she tried again.

She backed out of the room, bumping into the doorframe in her haste, and headed down the hallway. Her skin prickled, and she felt a flush spread down straight towards her chest. If she could just collect her thoughts. Good Lord, what must he think of her?

Jo suspected that she had stunned Mr. Wister—no, *Owen*—with her sudden exit, but he must have recovered himself more quickly than she was able to regain her own composure. He was only one or two steps behind her as she reached the door to her office.

"Wait! Are you okay?" he asked. "I'm so sorry if I've offended you somehow."

"No, I'm quite well, thank you," she tossed over her shoulder as she rushed through the doorway. She turned to close the door, but he'd already pushed halfway inside.

"All the same, shaking my hand doesn't normally make people physically ill. You'll excuse me for being a bit concerned about that."

He did seem concerned. Of course he did. He likely thought she was a madwoman.

The office was her sanctuary. The reassuringly solid presence of the oak desk and the Persian rug—worn now, but still one of the most colourful things in Fraser Springs—and the gooseneck brass lamp slowed her pulse. She breathed.

"I'm simply a bit overwarm, that's all. Please, don't trouble yourself."

She seated herself at her desk, partly to signal her eagerness to return to her work and partly to have an excuse to look anywhere other than at him. Her husband had towed the desk up to Fraser Springs by barge, paying enormous sums of money for the privilege of sitting behind it and staring at the springs as he worked. She tried to stare at the springs herself, to signal the end of the conversation. It was no use. Owen crossed the room to stand directly across from her.

"It's no trouble at all. Would you like me to fetch Miss Pedersen?" It took her a moment to realize that he meant Ilsa. She didn't think anyone had ever addressed Ilsa as "Miss Pedersen."

She sighed. "Mr. ... Owen, I don't need coddling, either from you or my employees. And this is my private office, so I would appreciate it if you'd return to one of the common areas until dinner." She picked up her best pen, tapped its nib against the side of the ink bottle, and nodded her head in the direction of the door.

He glanced around, as if only just realizing where they were. From inside their frames, four paintings of long-dead Wilson generations stared back at them. They all had Albert's kind eyes. And then Owen's eyebrows rose slightly. She followed his gaze. Damn. He had noticed the brick currently serving as a paperweight for the "love letters" she'd left spread out on the desk last night.

"Is that the brick that found its way through your front window?"

"Yes. I couldn't very well leave it on the floor." She pulled the big ledger closer, hoping to surreptitiously shuffle the letters out of sight.

The movement only served to draw his attention to the ragged stacks of clippings and creased letters. Before she could stop him, he reached across the desk and snatched one. She overcame the urge to slap his hand away as if he were a little boy stealing cake, and settled for directing her most suppressive scowl at him.

His focus, however, was firmly fixed on the paper.

"'How is the faithful city become a harlot! It was full of judgment; righteousness lodged in it; but now murderers,'" he read aloud, and looked up. "I assume that you are the 'now murderers'?"

"That"—she rose and snatched back the letter—"is none of your business. I know we've agreed to be more ... collegial, but that does *not* mean you may read my correspondence."

"If this is your correspondence, I think you should get some new pen pals," he replied as he plucked up another piece of paper, this time a clipping of cheap newsprint. "'This woman has ignored the warnings of good and decent people and flaunted her spiteful degeneracy,'" he read. "'Shall right-thinking citizens not drive out wickedness from their midst and cleanse the earth behind it?'"

Jo looked back at the portraits, reading disapproval in their painted eyes for the first time. Wickedness. Spiteful degeneracy. Harlots. This is what the name Wilson had come to mean.

"It's all talk," she said, as lightly as she could. "It's a small town with nothing better to do. They'll exhaust their vocabularies, get bored, and move on to the next crusade. This will all come to nothing."

"These aren't 'nothing'! These are attacks against your character. Death threats. Libel at the very least." He tossed down the scrap of paper on the pile. "How many of these are there?"

"Very few are death threats." She knew she was evading his question, but who did this man think he was? The cavalry riding in to rescue her from her tormentors? Truthfully, though, Jo felt relief mixed in with the ruffled feathers. He wasn't an employee who needed to be reassured by a facade of calm professionalism. He wasn't even really a client any longer. Whatever else he might be, he was at least an impartial witness, and someone for whom she had no reason to play the stoic. She sighed and sank back into her chair, rubbing her hands along the smooth armrests. The old leather absorbed the oil from her salved palms.

"Thirty-two. Thirty-three, counting the one from yesterday."

"The one that was delivered by way of a brick through your window." His words were blunt, but his tone was gentle.

Jo shook her head. It was hard to look at him but harder to look at the disapproving Wilsons on the walls. She sighed. "I don't know how it's gotten to this point. It started with the whispering after Albert passed. I thought it would blow over if I kept my head down and stayed committed to this place. But it didn't, and then all our employees left, and the St. Alice went up and took almost all of our tourist trade."

"So you brought in the girls. Which was rather savvy, by the way."

She nodded. "I don't regret it. It more than likely saved us. But it also gave the Society Ladies something to really sink their talons into. They want the old Fraser Springs whitewashed over and gone. Cultivating the wilderness! Filling the gambling dens with tea and hymns! And I gave them a perfect opening."

"*Ladies* wrote all of this?" He came around the desk to rifle through the papers again. She smiled ruefully at his baffled response to all the copperplate swoops and curlicues spelling out the foulest threats.

"The men know better," she explained. "They've been here, and they know there's nothing scandalous going on. Obviously, a few of them tried to take liberties when I first brought the girls on, but now they know we have rules here." She touched the curve of her eyebrow, trying to will away the headache forming there. She was tired. For the past two years, she'd been so incredibly, deeply tired.

"I'm doing my best. No, I'm doing *good* work here, and they refuse to see it. All these miners and loggers—their bodies are destroyed by their work. They're in pain. And I'm not a miracle worker, but we do untangle them, soothe their aches. We get them through another season at least." She paused. Had she ever said any of this out loud before? And when had Owen moved around to her side of the desk? She should go. This was becoming entirely too intimate.

She stood abruptly. The chair creaked behind her. Owen backed up a half step but no farther. "Those men are cowards. Someone should stand up for you."

His well-meaning condescension straightened her spine. "I've managed my own affairs for years now. I stand up perfectly well for myself." She stared him down, daring him to pity her.

"Yes," he agreed. "You certainly do." And he leaned across the space between them, placed his hand on her cheek, and kissed her.

Chapter 12

It was a ridiculous impulse. He had just expended every drop of his personal charm to convince her to let down her guard, only to immediately throw it away by acting like a mooning farm boy. But what had started as a reasonable admiration for her pluck and courage had been transformed the moment she'd risen, bringing those strange, bright eyes and flushed cheeks so close.

She inhaled sharply as his lips brushed hers. *Idiot*, a small rational voice shouted over the clamor of the rest of him. *She ran away from you for shaking her hand. She may not have shot you last night, but she certainly will now.* Too late.

She was fascinating. He *liked* her. He wanted her to like him. It was as simple and as complicated as that. Add to this the fact that she had spent the past two days touching him, thoroughly and systematically, and it was no wonder he was turned around. He would make this as chaste and quick a peck on the lips as he could, apologize profusely, and escape in whatever direction took him farthest from Jo Wilson until his head cooled.

He began to pull away, but then, miraculously, she stepped toward him, curling one of those sweet, work-roughened hands against his neck. Her lips parted, slightly but unmistakably, beneath his. He captured her other hand and pulled her the rest of the way against his body, which was suddenly alive with a thousand little vibrations at every point of their contact. He felt her sigh against his skin more than he heard it, and the last vestige of that small rational voice fell away.

Her fingers slid down his neck just as they had done only half an hour earlier in very different circumstances. Now, however, they grasped the fold of his unbuttoned collar, seeking to deepen the kiss, to bring her mouth closer to his. Her lips, firm and sure beneath his own, were even smoother than he'd imagined the night before. He brushed his thumb along her wrist and felt the smoothness there, too. She was softness and warmth. He breathed in her mint-and-talc smell. Even the faint fragrance of her perspiration was arousingly intimate. He tasted her lips, and the answering touch of her tongue against his sent a shiver through him.

The knock on the door seemed to be happening miles away. He ran his hand up her back to that glorious auburn hair, tangling his fingers in her curls, pulling at the pins there and ... the sound of a cough came from somewhere nearby. Startled, he released Jo and spun around to see Ilsa Pedersen doing a very poor imitation of sweet innocence.

"I'm so sorry; am I interrupting something?" She did not look one bit sorry. She looked, in fact, quite pleased.

Jo was flushed right down to her throat: from mortification or something more complimentary, he couldn't tell. Her hair had come loose—no, he had *pulled* it loose—and hung in soft wisps around her neck. The embarrassment he should have been feeling was tempered by his desire to plunge his fingers back into that hair, sweep it from her throat, kiss her again and again until she was back in his arms.

"Oh my goodness, Ilsa. I'm sorry. You're not interrupting. I was ..." She ran a hand over her hair, as if she could read his thoughts. "We need to get started in the kitchen. For supper."

Ilsa grinned. "Take your time. The potatoes will keep."

Owen searched Jo's face for a hint of her emotions. Her eyes darted around the room. He knew he should try to smooth this over, but he couldn't force the apology out of his mouth. He wasn't sorry. He didn't regret a single thing.

• • •

Jo looked at Owen. At Ilsa. At the framed Wilsons, the hate mail, the old wooden chair with the leather arms that her husband had so often sat back in. She was caught in the middle of a campaign to run her out of town for her lax morals, and she had allowed herself to be compromised in her own office.

She had to get out of the room. If she looked at Owen Sterling—at his mouth, at his eyes—she would be tempted all over again. What was wrong with her? With the door wide open and Ilsa or anybody else liable to walk in?

"I'm sorry," she said again, more firmly. "Ilsa, I'll be right down." She shifted her attention back to Owen. "And you can show yourself out." She barely registered the expression on his face as she took off upstairs to her bedroom, locking it behind her. Her heart was beating so loudly that she could hear it, could feel it pulsing in her neck and in her fingertips, and in her lips, which not five minutes ago had been so thoroughly kissed.

She poured water in the basin and splashed it on her face, but the coolness did not relieve the flush that thrummed through her skin. She touched her lips.

Stupid. It was stupid. She'd let her guard down, and this was exactly the wrong time for anything but steely resolve. The meeting was happening in just a few days, and she'd have to stand in front of the whole town and try to convince them that she was a chaste and virtuous widow who wasn't plotting to corrupt their community.

She was losing her mind. She breathed. She could set this right. She breathed again. She willed the flush in her cheeks to die down, willed slowness into her breath. She could do this. She could walk downstairs, smile at the patrons, chop onions, fry potatoes, add salt. She could grind the pepper, shine the cutlery, polish the residue from the water glasses, set the table. Running down these simple lists began to slow her pounding heart. She would light the stove, heft the cast-iron pans, check on the meatloaf. There, that was better.

She rearranged her hair for what felt like the millionth time that day, then touched a bottle of scent to her fingers and rubbed it to the back of her ears. Hadn't she just said to Owen—to Mr. Sterling—that people make mistakes? That they did the best they could? So she had made a mistake. It was a confusing, difficult time. She wouldn't let this ... whatever it was distract her.

Downstairs, she focused very intently on asking Susan about her day and Elsbeth about her mother, who was sick, and reminding Lucy to not slice the onions so thick, and tending the roux for the gravy. Jo enjoyed cooking: the way the lumps of flour dissolved into a glossy paste with the cream and butter, how the cheap cuts of meat became tender after hours of simmering. It was alchemy.

When the dinner service started, she was mostly relieved that Owen was absent. Hopefully, she hadn't made him think badly of her. Well, in truth, she didn't know what she wanted him to think or not think. A brief flash of panic came over her. What if he were simply using her to add colour to his article? A rakish tale of a gentleman traveler enjoying the favours of the bawdy local widow. Oh, God, her name could be in the papers!

"Breathe," Ilsa said softly, taking the pan of potatoes from Jo's hands and setting it on the table. She steered Jo towards the changing room. None of the miners seemed to notice, though as long as there was food on the table, they wouldn't notice the presence of a tap-dancing elephant.

Ilsa shut the changing room door behind them. "It's okay," she said. She was smiling.

"I'm sorry you had to see that," Jo said in the most professional tone she could muster. "It was a lapse in judgment, and it won't happen again. I'm supposed to set the example here."

Ilsa's smile was a soft, almost motherly expression. "It's okay," she said again. "It's not like you're strumping around after every man who comes past."

"I most certainly do not 'strump.' But with all that's happening, I can't afford a distraction. None of us can. I'm sorry. It was foolish of me."

Ilsa shrugged. "You've always had good judgment. So if you say that Mr. Wister isn't involved, then he isn't involved. And the more I talk to him, the more I see you're right: he's a terrible liar."

Jo smiled. "That's certainly true."

"Anyhow, if you want, I'll pretend the whole thing never happened and I never saw a thing. Certainly won't tell a soul."

"Yes, I'd appreciate that," Jo said. She hesitated. Feelings were difficult for her, expressing them even more so. "You're such a good ... Well. We can't keep dinner waiting. Shall we?"

Ilsa grinned and looped her arm with Jo's. "Let's."

Chapter 13

Owen Sterling gave precisely zero damns about what the towns-people would think of him for entering Doc Stryker's establish-ment at four in the afternoon. Hell, he would polka on the place's front porch if it meant getting a glass of liquor. He needed the burn of the raw whiskey to sear away the fog that had descended over his thoughts.

Nils Barson was lounging in one of the battered rockers on the porch. He looked up from his book as soon as Owen reached the stairs, but his wide smile evaporated under the influence of Owen's scowl.

"You okay, Mr. Wister?" Nils asked. Owen paused on the threshold.

"I will be shortly. Care to join me?" Nils shut the book and followed him in without a word.

Doc Stryker looked up from his ledger book as they came in. Even at this odd hour, a few old-timers were hunched over cards, though they seem to be playing for wooden plugs. They were all puffing on hand-rolled cigarettes of Lord knew what provenance, and the pungent odour somehow settled Owen's racing thoughts. In the dim daylight that sliced through the smoke, Owen could see that the bar was far smaller than he remembered. The floral wallpaper was so streaked with smoke residue that the outlines of the flowers were barely distinguishable from that of other stains. In the center of the room squatted an old potbelly stove, cold and unused because of the warm weather. No feminine touches or frippery anywhere, thank God. The bar was textured with knife cuts and carved inscriptions. *Joe loves Elsie*, he read. Lots of initials. A heart.

But this was no time to think of love or hunger or what a beautiful woman's mouth might have felt like pressed against his as her hair fell down around him. The time for reflection was over. He needed a drink.

"What can I get you fellas?" Doc Stryker asked. "House special?"

All the ornate bottles above the bar, he could see now, were filled with the same clear water. It would have to be the house special. "Make 'em doubles."

"Very good, sir," he said with a flourish, as if Owen had just ordered fine champagne. He lifted an amber jug from behind the bar and filled two generous glasses. "And what are we drinking to this afternoon, gentlemen? Money? Health? Love? Wine, women, and song?"

"Just toasting the end of another day," Nils said.

"Amen, amen to that," Doc Stryker said. Owen was sweating, despite the coolness of the room. "Surviving another day is about all we can ask for, now isn't it?"

The men at the back table grumbled their assent. Owen nodded. "Indeed."

"To surviving," Nils said.

"To surviving," the men repeated and slung back their own drinks.

The hooch worked its good magic: burning his throat, numbing his tongue to the lingering memory of Jo's mouth, and very likely vaporizing his nostril hairs so that they could not recall that talc and peppermint fragrance.

"'There cannot be good living where there is not good drinking,'" Owen quoted.

Doc Stryker grinned. "Ben Franklin, eh? Got us a scholar up here in the wilderness. Finally, someone who reads more than adventure stories about a boy and his dog."

"Hey," Nils exclaimed. "They aren't that bad." Owen was too distracted to feel properly insulted.

"Consummate works of art depicting the most basic struggle of man against nature—yes, yes, I know." He spread his hands along the bar and leaned towards them. "You know, I used to do some theatre back in my youth. Before I washed up here. Often thought I had a play or two in me to write what with my various travels, but the time gets away from you, doesn't it?"

"Everyone's got a story in them. You've just got to write it down," Owen said. *Hypocrite again.* He was, after all, fresh out of stories. What was he doing? He tapped the bar again. Time to incinerate all the introspection out of his brain.

"How you holding up, Doc?" Nils asked.

The little man's theatrical air deflated. It might have been the light coming in yellow through the tobacco-streaked windows, but he looked to have aged ten years since the night before. "Oh," he said, "we'll see, won't we?"

"You heard about Wilson's, eh?"

Doc Stryker sighed and filled up their glasses, pouring one for himself. They drank. "If the ne'er-do-wells who busted that window weren't most likely women, I would throw that brick right back at them. Hating me, I can understand. What with the devil's elixir"—he poured them another drink—"and the occasional game of chance among gentlemen." Even the miners grinned at that. "But Mrs. Wilson ..." He smiled ruefully. "'Envy breeds unkind division,' eh? Isn't that Shakespeare, Mr. Professor?"

"But she hasn't done anything to make anyone jealous," Owen said. "Not as far as I can see. The ladies she employs aren't ... improper."

Doc smirked. "Well, *you* know that. And I know that. But we all know that this town has four currencies. You've got your timber. You've got your ore. You've got your furs. And you've got gossip. Now, these ladies aren't chopping down trees, and they aren't swinging axes or skinning foxes, so what do they have left?

They started off trying to save the souls of this lot." He swung his thumb in the direction of the old-timers. "But it didn't quite work out the way they planned. But now they've found another cause to rally behind, and they're holding on for all they can get."

Nils downed his second—third?—drink. "Aw, Doc. We won't let anyone run you out."

Doc snorted. "Ain't nobody running me nowhere. I'm sixty-five years old. All the running's behind me. No, if anyone in this town wants me gone, they got to burn this place down with me in it, and that's that."

The drink and the good doctor's problems were beginning to put Owen's afternoon into perspective.

"It won't come to that, Doc," Nils said.

"What do you think Mrs. Wilson will do if they try to run her out of town?" Owen asked. As soon as he said it, he knew that the cheap liquor had gone straight to his head. He tried to rephrase the question. "I just mean, she's got no one, it seems. I hate to see a woman thrown out on her own like that."

Doc laughed. "Oh, Josephine Wilson's more than capable of taking care of herself. Don't you worry about her."

Nils seemed to be studying him. Owen looked away and tapped his fingers for another round. "Well, let's drink to you two! To Doc Stryker and Mrs. Wilson! Long may they reign!"

Doc poured the drinks. "It's bad luck to toast yourself. Let's just toast Mrs. Wilson."

"To Mrs. Wilson," the three men exclaimed as they raised their glasses.

Owen downed the drink. For years now, he'd done his damnedest to make his way in polite society, sipping tea at literary salons and learning to say witty things about fine wine and old brandy. So why did he still feel so comfortable downing hooch in this so-called bar, rubbing elbows with fur trappers and broken-down miners? Put him in a suit and a fine hat, and he'd still have the same rough edges. Oh well. It wouldn't hurt to let himself go for a few more days. High society could wait.

Chapter 14

Even in the moment, she knew she'd never go through with it. Still, just past midnight, Jo found herself spreading the scant contents of her life on her bed and packing them into a carpet bag she'd found in the storage room. She had made a mess of everything: of the bathhouse, of her husband's good name, of her own reputation. Best to simply hop a paddle wheeler to Vancouver and let Wilson's Bathhouse be swallowed back up by the wilderness. She could pawn her jewelry to get by until she got on her feet again. The girls would find other jobs. Mr. Sterling would go back to his comfortable life back in Vancouver.

She had no serious plans to leave, of course. She had committed herself to this place and to the girls, and she couldn't just go fleeing like some silly heroine. If nothing else, merely imagining the look of satisfaction on Mrs. McSheen's face as she declared victory over the murdering harlot was enough to keep Jo rooted. Still, the self-pity felt good.

She gently laid the tintype of her father down on the folded dresses, then picked it up again. He'd been only twenty or twenty-one when he'd had the photo taken as a souvenir during a carnival. The painted letters of the carnival's name had flaked away, but her father's young, unsmiling face remained on the metal. What had possessed a young man to spend his carnival money on posing somberly while the photographer fussed with the cordite powder rather than on sweets or sideshows was a question whose answer Jo would never know. It was just a bit of fun, he'd told her when she'd asked as a child. Now, it was the only image she had left of her father, who had never indulged in such fun again.

Strange to think that she'd never met this version of her father in person. She hadn't been born until he was thirty-four. Jo couldn't connect the cold, grey eyes of the young man staring, ramrod straight, off at some horizon with the portly, red-faced father who had raised her alone after her mother passed. She had no photographs of her mother, and Jo's father had rarely spoken about her. Somehow, the absence of any personal relics made her seem like a character from a story. Just another young bride perishing in childbirth, gone before she got a chance to see her baby's face.

It was too late for morbid thoughts or childish escape fantasies. Jo unpacked it all: her three dresses that weren't work costumes, the jewelry Albert had given her, the tintype. She brushed out her hair, braided it, and set the tintype of her father back on the bedside table. Maybe if she stared at the photograph long enough, she would dream of him and she could explain everything: how sorry she was, how she didn't know what to do, how she wasn't sure how to make the money last through the season even if she wasn't run out on the next rail. She stared so long that the afterimage of her father's face floated on her vision when she looked away.

Her dreams refused to listen to her plan. Instead, Owen Sterling invaded her sleeping mind again. At first, they were back in her office. He kissed her gently. She tried to deepen the kiss, but he wouldn't let her. His lips just brushed against hers so that the roughness of his stubble grazed her chin. He tilted her head back with one hand and kissed her chin. Then her neck. When he reached the high, ruffled collar of her dress, he unbuttoned the first button and kissed the newly exposed skin. Removed another button. Kissed the half-inch of skin he revealed. He moved so slowly, so deliberately, that she wanted to beg him to hurry.

And then, in the strange logic of dreams, they were no longer in the office but in the empty bathhouse. The light from the vertical windows striped their bodies with sun and shade. They were both luminous with sweat from the bathhouse's humidity. Though they were naked, she felt no shame. The door, she sensed, was locked, and only the half-ruined faces of the Greek figures on the tiles could see them. Nothing could possibly be wrong. He was straddling her, and she strained with him.

Suddenly, she was watching the entire scene unfold as if from above. The sun stippled their naked bodies in hazy yellow light, and his back muscles tensed and relaxed as he plunged into her. She wrapped her legs around his waist and was not afraid to cry out—

She woke suddenly. It was pre-dawn, and the light through the window was weak and pale rather than the warm gold of her dream. The sheets and quilt were tangled around her, as if she'd been twisting and turning in her sleep. She felt too relaxed to be ashamed or frustrated. Instead, she lay in bed for several long moments, enjoying the last of the sensations coursing through her.

Maybe a titillating dream was all she needed to shake out that silliness. Owen was handsome, yes. And he was charming, absolutely. And he was a *distraction*: the last thing she needed right now. Invigorated, she climbed out from under the too-warm bedclothes and padded down the stairs in her robe.

Even in the steely light streaming from the high windows, Jo knew the bathhouse by heart. She stripped off her nightgown and entered the warm water to enjoy her bath. The room lightened around her, and the bathhouse walls were tinged with pink and orange as dawn broke. She luxuriated in the warm water, feeling totally calm, completely in control again. As she washed her hair, a plan formed. There was no need for unpleasantness. She would just delay the discussion with Owen until after the meeting. She was sorry, she would say, but she had too many responsibilities for ... whatever this was.

She would assign Annie to see to Owen, and then she'd spend the day making a public show around the town. Would a politician hide away when he was campaigning? No, of course not. So why should Jo Wilson cower in her bathhouse while the Society Ladies slandered her up and down the boardwalk? No, she would put on her church dress and go greet every scowl with a smile. *Why, hello there, Mr. Evans. Haven't seen you with us for awhile. Good morning, Mrs. McSheen. How lovely to see you today. What's that? Why of course I would like one of your leaflets!*

She would prove that Jo Wilson was no shrinking violet, and then she would show up at the meeting with the same resolve: perfectly in control, completely focused. Owen Sterling would have to wait.

Chapter 15

The shriek of dozens of forks and knives against plates was not helping Owen's hangover one bit, nor was the sight of chewed food in open mouths or crumbs in beards. Owen's fellow diners clearly prioritized speed over elegance when it came to table manners. He looked down at his plate, trying to focus on the fact that the coffee was hot and the bacon at Wilson's could soothe any malady, but he couldn't seem to pull his attention away from the dozens of chewing mouths. Like cows lined up in the feedlot. With the window still blocked off, the only light seemed to come from the lamps glinting off bread-crusted teeth.

The only cheering thought was that Jo would arrive and he would be able to apologize, an act that would calm his stomach more than the bread and bacon. After returning to the St. Alice, he'd spent an hour formulating an eloquent, sincere apology for his ungentlemanly behaviour, an apology that would mollify Jo while leaving the situation open to further kisses. Unfortunately, he'd woken up this morning with a pounding headache and not one recollection of the genius that had apparently coursed through him last night. His head throbbed so much that the edges of the room seemed to pulse along with his heartbeat.

Across from him, two men argued about the outcome of a recent poker game, and several more shared their own opinions about what fate should befall no-good cheaters. The room was humid and fragrant with the smell of bacon grease, bread, and coffee. He'd opted to wear one of the double worsted banker's outfits he'd been loaned and was regretting the decision as he felt the first beads of sweat slide down between his shoulder blades.

It seemed that all of Fraser Springs had crammed into this small, dim room for the sole purpose of arguing and chewing with their mouths open. In fact, the only person who appeared to be missing was Jo. Maybe she had slept late, as she had done before. Still, as the meal was cleared away and the patrons wandered off for treatments or work, Owen tried to figure out how to inquire about her.

"Mr. Wister?" Ilsa asked. Having shed the name in front of Jo, Owen had forgotten that he hadn't outed himself to the rest of Fraser Springs. "Mr. Wister?" she said again.

"Oh, I beg your pardon. What is it?"

"You can take your bath treatment whenever it's convenient. Your attendant is waiting."

"Ah. Well, I didn't see Mrs. Wilson here, so I thought ..."

She gave him a thin smile. "I'm sorry, but Mrs. Wilson is indisposed today. She's very busy with the meeting coming up, but Annie is one of our best attendants."

This time, it wasn't the hangover causing his stomach to flop. His faint nausea was burned away by anger. So she wasn't even going to let him explain? She was just going to ignore him as if he were some kind of embarrassment? Would she hole up somewhere until he left?

Owen forced a smile. "I'm sure she's excellent," he said.

Annie may have been excellent. She may have been terrible. She may have been the fabled man-beast they called the Sasquatch for all Owen noticed. He sat in the steaming bath focusing intently on the beads of sweat rolling down his forehead and neck until they joined the water as the other patrons swapped stories around him.

Jo's ignoring him wasn't right, and it certainly didn't match the picture he'd conjured of her in his mind. Last night, he'd lain awake and wondered if she, too, was unable to sleep. Perhaps her thoughts were also roiling like the fizzling waters: a melodramatic comparison generated by Doc Stryker's hooch, he could see. Maybe those guarded grey eyes weren't guarded at all. They were just cold, a door to nothing.

But maybe she was just running an errand. She probably didn't trust herself to act naturally around him in the company of others and so was waiting for a time when they could speak in private. It seemed likely. Alone in the treatment room, she would be standoffish at first, but before long ... Well, she'd kissed him back, hadn't she? He'd been surprised at her passionate response; at the way she'd gripped his collar.

The scent of mint in the bathhouse was a constant reminder of her.

Annie inquired if there was anything else she could help him with. As politely as he could, he informed her that there was not. Her white dress made her look like a ghost, and she moved spectrally at the edge of his vision, folding towels and fussing after other clients. He was being unkind to her, he knew, but between the headache and Jo's absence, he couldn't help but be standoffish.

After the bath, he wandered to the treatment room, trying to patch together a workable monologue, but the words became a jumble of clichés and maudlin phrases that one of the characters in his books might say. *My boldness was misguided, but my intentions were pure.* No. That sounded like something a politician would say. *I got caught up in the moment and I thought*— No, that made it seem like a mistake when it wasn't.

He removed his shirt, lay down on the enameled tin table, and pressed his head against the cool metal, which soothed his hangover. The window was open, and a faint breeze stirred against the sweat on his back. *I hope I didn't startle you, but I, for one, greatly enjoyed what transpired between us, and I hope ...* No, it was all wrong. He would just have to take his cue from Jo when she arrived.

But when the door opened, it was Annie again. The disappointment on his face must have been apparent, because the girl looked as if she might cry. She was only a girl. She was trying her best. He was being unkind.

"Have I upset you somehow, Mr. Wister?" she asked. "I'm so sorry if I have."

"No, no, of course not. I was lost in thought, and you startled me." He offered her a smile. "I look forward to our treatment."

Annie's small, callused hands tried hard to trace down the source of his tension, but it was clear that either she did not have the hand strength, or the source of his tension could simply not be remedied by massage. It was out there, somewhere in Fraser Springs, hiding from him.

He'd blown it. Or she'd blown it. What was her plan? To run this place into the ground until the St. Alice swallowed up all the remaining business, the mines ran dry, and the clients went elsewhere? And then what?

The muscles in his neck were taut with aggravation now, no matter how Annie's little hands worked. His headache grew. The thing was—the thing that Jo just didn't understand—was that she could only hide from her problems for so long. Eventually, she'd have to face them head on. And Owen wasn't even a problem, for God's sake. If a man falling for her was a problem, well, then she'd had a pretty charmed life.

Falling for her. The massage had ended without Owen's noticing, and he was suddenly alone in the room. *Was* he falling for her? It was far too soon for that kind of foolishness. He wasn't some swooning romantic to go moon-eyed for a lady on two days' acquaintance. Hell, he'd always been the kind to cut and run when things showed signs of getting serious. And what, exactly, did he want to get out of this? Well, none of it mattered now. She'd cut him off in one, ice-cold swoop. She didn't want to even *talk* to him about what happened.

No, she was certainly *not* being fair to him. He washed off the oil in the bathing room, dried off, and dressed. As he walked back to the St. Alice, the humidity instantly slickened his skin. Why should Jo be the only one who had a say in all this? He would track her down tonight, and they'd have it out. Chances were good that she would never want to see him again, but at least he would know. Better that than this agony of waiting.

Nothing was going according to plan. For years, he had told himself that he would settle down after his career was established: when he was not just a popular children's writer, but a *success*. Success, then marriage. He'd courted a few women in his time, of course. But after a certain point, he'd always sensed that they liked him *even though*. Even though he didn't come from an old family. Even though his permanent address was a boarding house. Even though he'd had to buy his typewriter on credit. They'd never *said* as much, but once those suspicions had crept in, the connection had never seemed to last.

At least Jo had an established business to her name. What did he have beyond decent looks and a monthly royalty check that rose and fell unpredictably? No, he wasn't going to make any promises to a woman until he had something solid to offer her. It hurt his pride to admit it, but Jo might be right to keep him at arm's length.

Chapter 16

There was no need for armour when you had a perfectly pressed and starched dress. Not to mention the tortoiseshell comb, the brilliantly shined shoes, the modest neckline secured with a cameo brooch, the drop of rosewater behind the ears. Would carrying a Bible be too much? Yes. She didn't need to hide behind anything.

The town of Fraser Springs was built on a hill sloping down towards the water, so all the houses seemed to be peering their noses down at the people walking along the town's main boardwalk. Jo loved the sound her feet made on the planks. Confident. Purposeful. The calls of the seabirds, the sloshing of the water against the wharf: it all combined in a soothing rhythm she'd grown to love during the past five years.

Even at this early morning hour, townspeople were going about their business. Today was Thursday, and that meant the SS *Minto* would be docking soon, dropping off passengers and crates and collecting letters and goods bound for market in Vancouver. Already, a crowd of people milled by the long wharf, waiting for whatever news the boat would bring.

Jo slipped inside the general store. Ilsa usually did the shopping, so it had been more than a month since she'd smelled its familiar mélange of dust and nutmeg, dried fish, and licorice. Jo's eyes adjusted to the light as she surveyed the barrels of dry goods, the long ropes of garlic hanging from the ceiling and swaying in the thick air, the bolts of fabric, the glass cases selling everything from boiled sweets to liver tonic to spectacles. When she'd first moved to Fraser Springs, she had taken her father to the store, and they'd made a game of trying to identify the strangest thing in the shop and guess who might buy it. She'd won with elbow-length work gloves made from a pair of bear paws.

"I don't know," her father had said, grinning. "Maybe some American fellow is very serious about his right to 'bear arms.'"

Even now, Jo groaned at her father's joke. She looked up to find the clerk's helper staring at her. He was a lanky teenaged boy who she didn't recognize.

"How would I go about getting some plate glass shipped in?" she asked him.

"Oh, I don't ... uh... I don't—" the assistant stammered. Either he was utterly green, or her reputation had preceded her.

Jo gave her best, most patient smile. "Could you ask your employer? My front window broke, and I need to replace it."

"If you didn't have those miners horsing around at all hours, you wouldn't have so much damage," said a clerk, coming out from the storeroom behind the counter. He was a wiry little man with a moustache so well groomed it looked drawn on.

Again, Jo forced the smile and the calm voice. "Oh, it wasn't the miners' fault. Someone was merely trying to deliver me a message and missed my letterbox." She smiled. "Accidents happen, you know."

The clerk and his assistant both reddened.

"That kind of shipment's a special order, ma'am, I'm not sure we could manage it," the clerk said.

"I've placed special orders here previously. Have you discontinued the practice?"

The clerk looked down at the glass cases. Up at her. "Well, it's just that we only allow special orders for... distinguished creditors, such as your late husband." He composed himself enough to meet her gaze. "A small establishment such as ours can't afford to place a special order and then have payment default. It would ruin us.

And a breakable item like glass? Well, it just can't be done." The clerk was in full form now: his posture was ramrod straight, as was his moustache. "No, I'm sorry, ma'am, but it just cannot be managed."

She stared evenly at him. "How would you recommend I go about getting the glass to fix my window?"

The clerk's mouth twitched at the corner. "My advice, ma'am? You wait to see the results of the meeting. No sense worrying yourself trying to place an order if you don't plan to stay out the season."

Jo channeled her anger into a posture rigid enough to match his and took a breath. "You've received some incorrect information, sir. I fully intend on staying out the season, and all the seasons after. Although, come to think of it, I *will* be taking a day trip to Nelson after this meeting to speak with the special constable there about the unfortunate number of window breakages my business has been suffering. I've also got some letters he may want to take a look at." She did not wait to see the clerk's reaction. Instead, she gave his underling a winning smile and headed for the door.

"Have a good day, ma'am," the clerk called after her. "I'm sure I'll see you tomorrow."

Normally, a confrontation like that would leave Jo with a pounding heart, but all she felt was a cool, deep calm. She was beyond anger now. Just twenty-four more hours of smiling sweetly and she would have a chance to defend herself. She headed towards the dock, where the SS *Minto* was coming in. Usually, she loved to watch the big boat glide into the harbour, loved the way the paddlewheel churned waves that slapped rhythmically against the dock, loved all the hopeful people awaiting visitors, parcels, and mail. Today, however, she felt only the same calm chill through her body.

"Hello," she said, greeting each person she recognized in the crowd. "Good morning."

A hushed murmur rippled through the townspeople as she approached, but she maintained her decorum and her posture.

"Looking to get on the next boat out of here?" someone jeered.

"No, actually. Just enjoying the view." She turned to give the person who spoke a smile, but whoever it was had melted back into the crowd. "And reminding disembarking passengers that I'm offering a sale this weekend. All spa treatments for two cents."

"Two cents is all your girls are worth." Another female voice.

Though she felt the ligaments in her neck might snap from all the forced smiling, she was fully prepared to do this all day. "My girls are very well trained, and I'm proud of their work." She sounded like a brochure, but it was good to have a script at times like this. "You're welcome to come and try our services to see if you agree."

That seemed to quiet them. Out of insults, they made a point of ignoring her. Jo glimpsed Mrs. McSheen in the crowd, consulting with her fellow Society Ladies. "How do you do, Mrs. McSheen," she called out, waving merrily at them. The SS *Minto* gave a long, low hoot to signal its arrival. "And hello Mrs. Campbell and Mrs. Gunnerson and Mrs. Avery." The group of women looked up like startled birds.

"It's so good to see you," Jo said. "Such lovely weather we're having, isn't it?"

The women reddened, trapped by their social obligation to make polite small talk. "We'll see you at the meeting," Mrs. McSheen finally managed, and the women huffed off to dissect the encounter over tea in the St. Alice.

And so it went. All morning and well into the late afternoon, her posture so straight it would make a deportment teacher proud, her voice calm and sweet, her neck and shoulders tense from the effort of maintaining her facade. Well, at least she had shown that she wasn't afraid. And though she could have been imagining it, some of the townspeople did seem to soften towards her. It was, after all, easier to hate a faceless harlot who never left her den of iniquity than it was to hate the lady politely inquiring about the price of your cabbages or asking whether your baby was over his croup.

Jo followed the wooden boardwalk back to the bathhouse but veered off before she got to the front door. Winding her way along a barely perceptible path past the miners' cabins and down a rocky outcropping, she eventually arrived at the one safe, private place she had in the town.

She had discovered the grotto in her first few months in Fraser Springs. It was a sanctuary she had never shared with anyone: not her father, not Albert, not the girls. The townspeople must be too busy building hotels up towards the sky to bother looking down, or they would flock to this place. Even in the humidity, the small grotto was cool; its water was never as hot as the main springs. In the evenings, the last light of the day flooded in from fissures in the rock, spangling across the white limestone. All around her, pale rock whorled in frozen waves and twisting spires, like a cathedral shaped by God's own hands. It smelled of moss and wet stone, its mineral waters steaming gently into the cooling air of dusk. Had she chosen to speak, her voice would have echoed hugely, but she preferred silence in the grotto. The water burbling and tapping against the stone was the only sound she needed.

Jo unpinned her hair and let it fall down her back. She placed the comb and the brooch on a little ledge formed by the rock, then struck life into a mismatched assortment of half-melted candles and wax stubs she kept there in anticipation of the darkness that would arrive in an hour or so. She unbuttoned her shirtwaist, skirt, and petticoats, and slid out of them. After days spent buttoned into stifling wool, the chilled air was delightful. On the hottest days, she sometimes imagined that the limestone grotto was an ice palace or a snow castle. Freed of the skirt's weight, her chemise ruffled against her legs.

Jo brushed the leaves and burrs from her skirt and placed her clothes carefully on the limestone shelf. She had no fear of anyone seeing her in her underthings. In five years, no one had ever ventured down to the grotto, though the paintings of handprints and men chasing horses she found when she explored farther into the cave's depths suggested that the place had known visitors in the past. She loved the fluid lines of the images, the way the horses and men seemed to bend around the limestone's curves.

Jo slipped into the water. Steam curled in little eddies across the surface, and the contrast of the hot water with the chill on her face and neck soon relaxed her. The limestone had been worn smooth by the almost imperceptible current of water and felt like ceramic against her bare skin.

Although the water here lacked the potency of what they piped through the bathhouse, it still fizzled faintly against her body. She closed her eyes, listening to the *pat, pat, pat* of the water droplets echoing across the grotto's hollows. Her heartbeat slowed to the droplets' cadence. *Pat, pat, pat.* Her mind felt as blank and white as the limestone walls. Owen Sterling, Mrs. McSheen, the rude clerk ... they all drifted away.

As the water lapped against her body, however, thoughts of Owen crept insistently into the stillness. She couldn't imagine what he must think of her right now. It had surely been terribly rude of her to simply vanish without any explanation, but there was nothing to be gained from allowing herself to be distracted from her commitment to Wilson's. This was not the time to behave like a silly girl whose head had been turned by a handsome face and a single kiss.

Running the bathhouse was difficult, especially with the recent groundswell of malicious gossip, but it was the one place where she truly felt in control. It had taken her years to learn the business, but now her bookkeeping was tidy, her staff was well trained, and her clientele was small but fiercely loyal. The issue of the broken window was tricky, but she would figure something out. At Wilson's Bathhouse, problems always seemed to have an answer. Every day, she choreographed three huge and flawless meal services, played peacemaker to spats between the girls, healed a half-dozen aching bodies, repaired loose boards and frayed towels and leaking washtubs with her own hands, and then went to bed with the satisfaction of a job well done.

Then again, she always went to bed alone. For the first time since Albert's passing, she was beginning to suspect that might be a problem as well. She wouldn't have responded to Owen Sterling with such intensity if she were truly satisfied with a life of virtuous celibacy. But Owen was not the solution to that problem; he was an entire barrel of *new* problems. Nevertheless, her stomach clenched at the idea that he might be angry with her. He'd been so kind, and now he was probably packing, cursing himself for getting involved with such a capricious woman. She'd likely never see him again.

Chapter 17

He looked for her in the bathhouse, at the general store, at the wharf, even at Doc Stryker's bar, but Jo Wilson seemed to have vanished into the mists. It was doubtful that she was cowering in her bedroom, but it seemed the only logical explanation. Perhaps he'd read her wrong. Perhaps her spitfire boldness only applied to her business affairs.

It was only by chance that he finally saw her. He happened to be outside, walking along the lakeshore to clear his thoughts: sulking, if he was being truly honest. Jo strode right past him, seeming completely lost in thought. He was about to call out to her, when she turned sharply left, into the bushes. What in heaven's name was she doing tromping through the underbrush?

He watched as she wove her way past the miners' cabins behind the bathhouse and into the trees, following a path even a deer couldn't have deciphered. Suddenly, she dropped out of sight, as if the earth had simply swallowed her. For a long moment, he hesitated at the edge of the woods. Mosquitos droned all around him. He was certainly not going to go charging after the woman, crashing through the undergrowth, just to demand an apology. All the same ... He swore under his breath as he pushed into the trees. This damned town and this damned woman would make a fool of him yet.

The humidity intensified the fragrance of sage and sap-swollen fir trees. As he walked in the general direction Jo had gone, he saw trees, so big that two men couldn't have gotten their arms around them, clinging crazily to rocky outcroppings and gnarling their roots around half-exposed boulders. He'd have to come back with better shoes to explore, maybe do a few rough sketches of the geography for a future novel. Not that he intended to write another one, of course. But being out at the edge of the wilderness made him imagine all sorts of convenient calamities that could befall a hero. He could be climbing and slip on a mossy rock. A freak blizzard could blow through, and he'd have to cleave to one of these massive trees for shelter. He could—

Owen stopped just in time to avoid skittering down a steep creek bed. He could break his own fool neck, is what could happen to his hero. He looked more closely at the rock fall. A scrape of dark turned earth and the sharp smell of broken pine twigs alerted him to the fact that someone had scrambled down it recently.

He made his way down the rocks, following the creek along its course. After a few yards, a little waterfall tumbled down from the top of the far bank. Over its rushing chatter, he could hear the oddly echoing sound of lapping water. There must be ... yes, there was an opening behind the falls. A moment later, as his vision adjusted to the dim light, he found himself surrounded by pale limestone and running water.

Owen had scaled mountains and glaciers, had hiked into volcanic calderas, had swum in the open ocean, but he'd never been in a place like this. He touched the walls and found them damp and cool; the stone had the lambent gleam of beeswax. The anger and irritation he'd been cultivating all day began to deflate and drain away, soothed by the sound of the running water and the loveliness of the smooth, white stone. Faintly, he heard little splashes coming from somewhere ahead, their source hidden by a sharp bend in the stone.

He had followed Jo to apologize, to scold, to let her know that he wasn't going to be ignored any longer. Now the idea of speaking at all seemed foolish. It was as if he had wandered into a strange church, in the middle of a holy service conducted in some language he did not understand. He took a few more quiet steps into the cool grotto and suddenly saw the warm, yellow flicker of refracted candlelight.

Jo.

She floated serenely in the still blue water of the grotto. She was undressed; water sluiced off her shoulders and breasts, which were visible under the wet fabric of her slip.

She should have seemed vulnerable in her nakedness. Instead, he felt as he did when he came upon a wild animal confident in the sanctity of its own lair. There was that same breathless pause as he waited for her to register his presence, and flee.

It seemed as if he had been standing there for an hour or more, and still Jo Wilson appeared to be completely oblivious to his presence. Perhaps he was in the shadows. Perhaps she was ignoring him. He should leave, and yet he stood transfixed. Good God, what a fine woman. Her skin was paler in the light reflecting off the cave walls, her hair floating free and loose around her. The water was almost unnaturally blue.

She ducked under the water and quickly bobbed back to the surface. Owen smiled at this evidence of playfulness from the stubbornly starched Mrs. Jo Wilson. She was a seal, perhaps, or an otter—some sleek and lovely water creature that would look him straight in the eye and then simply slip away from him with barely a ripple.

A moment's pause, and she was back under the water. Owen waited for her to break the surface once more. Another minute passed without so much as a ripple. Obviously the woman could swim, but he doubted she was a pearl diver, able to hold her breath so long. He shifted uneasily, and his heart began to pound. After another long minute with no sign of her—not even a bubble—he kicked off his shoes, shrugged out of his coat, and waded in after her.

. . .

From the little stone hollow on the other side of the underwater passage, Jo heard loud splashing in the outer grotto. A fish? No, the sound was far too loud. Good Lord, another *person*? She ducked quickly back through the little channel. As she broke up to the warmer air of the main pool, she saw Owen Sterling, soaking wet, his eyes wide and his face drained of colour.

"Jo!" he barked. In this small quiet space, his voice was like a gunshot. She startled and lost her footing a bit on the smooth stone. She ducked and spluttered as he caught at her arm and pulled her upright.

"Owen! What on earth?" He drew closer; the wake of his movement washed against her. She suddenly remembered that she was practically naked and clamped her free arm across her chest.

"Have you lost your mind? Are you all right?" he demanded.

"No! I mean, yes. Yes, of course I'm all right." She shook her arm free of his grasp and pulled away. "Were you *following* me?"

"You disappeared!"

"I did not 'disappear.' There's another little cave just through there." She waved vaguely.

"That's not what I meant. You've been avoiding me all day."

"What? I was not avoiding you. I was *busy*. Campaigning for Wilson's. Perhaps you're too self-absorbed to remember that I have a business to run."

That was too much—she almost flinched as soon as the words left her mouth.

"*Busy?*" he spat. "You think I'll believe that it's pure coincidence that after I kissed you, you decided to spend all day campaigning like a two-bit politician? After we'd agreed to carry on just as before?"

"It's better than slinking around feeling sorry for myself. I refuse to be distracted by ..." She looked down at the water, then up at him again. She tried to focus on his face, not the contours of his strong shoulders, visible through the wet fabric of his shirtsleeves. "I refuse to look back a year from now and say, 'If only I hadn't lost focus, if only I'd tried a little harder, if only I hadn't hidden away and let people slander me.'" The stone walls amplified her rising voice until it sounded like she was shouting from a megaphone. "So, yes, I suppose I was ignoring you."

There was an awkward silence then. Neither she nor Owen seemed quite sure where to look.

"Did you really think I would drown in four feet of water?" she asked, finally.

"If I'd known it was only four feet of water, I wouldn't have made such an ass of myself," he replied. "In fact, I'd very much appreciate it if we can agree that when you tell this story, I saved your life." His rueful smile was as good an olive branch as any.

"It serves you right for sneaking after me, at any rate."

"Yes. I am thoroughly chastened."

"Well. As long as you're chastened, you may as well take the two-penny tour." She reached across the space between them and took his hand. He looked startled for a moment—the water had hidden her motion—and then he allowed her to draw him along to the far wall.

"Am I to understand that you have a secret grotto inside of a secret grotto?"

"Of course. All the most fashionable ladies do. We just duck under and through and we're there. You'll want to close your eyes. The water stings a bit if you don't. And watch your head." He nodded and tightened his grip on her hand. Down, under, through, and up.

The water was shallower and cooler, and the light much dimmer. The view, however, was stunning. Baroque arabesques and whorls of limestone swirled down from the roof and along the walls, pristinely and startlingly white. As Owen surfaced beside her, she watched his reaction carefully, even though she could barely see him. It felt important, somehow, that he appreciate this place. He stood silently and did not let go of her hand. She ruffled the water around her thigh with her free hand.

At last, he let out a long breath. "I spent all of today rehearsing ways to tell you that kissing you yesterday was a mistake, and that I regret it. But it wasn't, and I don't. That may make me the worst bounder in the Northwest, but I am not sorry I kissed you, Jo Wilson. And I don't want to pretend that my interest in you is purely professional." She felt more than saw him move closer to her. He skimmed his slick hands up her arms, gently and almost tentatively, as if she were a skittish horse.

She had never met anyone like this man. He seemed so sure of himself in the rough-and-tumble world of outdoorsmen and so charmingly at sea everywhere else. He smiled and laughed freely, and he made her smile and laugh, too. She barely knew him, but she closed her eyes, savoring the touch of his hands along her skin. It had been so long since she'd been touched like this. If he wanted to hurt her—if he was still after a juicy story and thought he could get a little lovemaking in the bargain— he could simply join the queue of her ill-wishers. Things had been going so wrong for so long. She needed to let herself believe that something would go right. That everything could be as simple as letting Owen Sterling kiss her.

She placed her own hands on his chest, and Owen inhaled sharply. His arms slipped around her waist, and their lips met. That first kiss in her office had been sudden, a rush of surprise and jangling response. This, though, felt inevitable. Their bodies fit together so beautifully. They took their time, exploring the contours of each other's lips. The kiss deepened slowly, incrementally, until they were both breathing in little moans, their hands impossibly tangled in and under their wet clothing.

Owen, finally, broke the kiss and rested his forehead against hers. She raised her hand to brush along the rough stubble of his jaw, and he leaned the weight of his head into her touch. He seemed almost as hungry for tenderness as she was. He pressed his lips into the cup of her hand, and she laughed, feeling suddenly giddy. She felt his answering grin against her palm before he pulled back to look at her.

"My God, Jo," he said. His voice was ragged around the edges. "I think we need to get back to dry land before I lose the ability to walk."

She laughed again and led him back under and out into the candlelit main grotto. Together, they half-swam, half-splashed across to the wide rock ledge where their clothes lay, Jo's in a neat stack, Owen's coat crumpled in a hasty pile.

He pulled himself up onto the ledge and turned to take her hand and haul her up after him. Her mouth went dry; the way his soaking shirt and trousers clung to his body, he might as well have been nude. The evidence of his desire for her was unmistakable. A wave of basely physical need tightened across her stomach and between her thighs. Lord, perhaps she *was* lost to feminine modesty and decorum after all. Still, with Owen's wide, openhearted smile, it was impossible to feel properly depraved.

Jo took his hand and joined him on the ledge. In the candlelight and without the sheer veil of the water, she felt suddenly exposed and reflexively drew her loose, wet hair across her bosom. Owen reached across her and brushed it back behind her shoulders.

"Let me look at you, Jo," he said.

"Don't you like a lady to have a bit of mystery?"

"But you've got something better than a bit of mystery."

She raised her eyebrows. "And that is?"

"You've got me, of course," he pronounced with an exaggerated seriousness that was undermined by the glint in his eyes. He smothered her response with another kiss, drawing her tightly against his chest. Playfulness quickly became something more as his hands and lips roamed across her body, teasing and stroking and caressing.

The cool air of the grotto began to raise goose bumps on her arms. Her wet chemise suddenly felt clammy.

"Owen," she gasped. "We're going to catch pneumonia."

"Mmm hmm," he agreed, his face nuzzling into the tender space between her neck and shoulder.

"We should ... oh! We have to get out of our wet ... things."

That got his attention. Almost before she could finish the thought, he was bare-chested, his eager hands rucking the soaking-wet chemise up around her thighs, her hips, up over her head.

She did her best not to blush or hide herself from his gaze. "Jo," he breathed as he drew her slowly against him, skin against warm skin for the first time. "You are so beautiful."

They didn't speak again until she reached behind him and pulled her carefully folded skirts and petticoats into a frothy pile at their feet. Owen's eyes widened at the silent invitation. Feeling bolder and more brazen than ever before in her life, she let her hands trail down the golden-brown hair of his torso to the straining buttons of his trousers. "You still seem to be overdressed."

She fumbled with the closures for a moment before Owen took over. Freed, his cock jutted hard between them; she reached for it and stroked along its hot length once, slowly. Owen groaned in the back of his throat and pulled them both down atop her tumbled skirts. "Not yet. You'll kill me if you keep touching me like that." Even as he said this, though, he slid his own fingers between her legs.

She closed her eyes and surrendered to the sensation of his strong, sure fingers parting her folds, searching for the center of the yearning ache that was radiating through her body. Her back arched as his tongue lapped at her breasts, circling her swollen, tender nipples. A low, animal moan escaped her as she felt herself tighten and coil around the places where Owen teased and licked and fondled. She began to writhe against his hand.

"Yes, Jo. Show me."

One endless moment later, the orgasm broke over her, and she called out wordlessly before she sank back into the warm reality of Owen's body against hers. He kissed her deeply before he lifted himself up over her. She wrapped her legs around his hips and sighed as she felt his cock probe gently between her legs. She lifted to meet him—how easily they moved together—and he paused. His question was unspoken but clear: was this too far?

"Please," she gasped, softly. Her heart was beating so hard that her fingertips pulsed. He closed his eyes and sank his head against the curve of her neck. Even though she had not made love in more than four years, she felt no pain when he entered her, only a rush of sensation as his cock filled her. She gripped his back as he thrust and stroked, her fingers following the familiar hard planes of the muscles there. This time, however, their roles had reversed. He was the one finding sources of tension, building it up with each stroke until they were both incoherent with need. She clung to him as, finally, the force of his climax slammed through him, sweeping her along into her own white-hot oblivion.

They lay there, spent and entangled, until the last of the mismatched candles began to gutter.

• • •

Darkness had fallen by the time Owen walked Jo back to Wilson's. They'd dressed in candlelight, their clothes still damp. He'd tried to lend a hand with the complicated series of undergarments and dresses that made up a modern woman's outfit. Dresses over dresses over more dresses, all fastened with fiddly little hooks and clasps and buttons.

"I'm surprised women don't need a university degree just to get dressed in the morning," he said.

She smiled. "And you thought you had it rough with your wool suits." She attempted to brush the wrinkles from her shirtwaist. "I'll have to get this pressed before tomorrow." She grimaced.

"Ah," he said. "I almost forgot about tomorrow." The word lingered in the air. Even the magic of this place couldn't banish reality forever.

She dismissed the word with a wave of the hand. "Tomorrow will come soon enough," she said. "And what will happen will happen." She tied the bow at her throat and tried to twist her curls into some semblance of order. "There."

He smiled at her. Even in wrinkled, half-sodden clothing, she was so beautiful. "Did you bring a lantern?" he asked. She was snuffing the last valiant little candle, and its smoke twisted in a little spiral that mimicked the stalactites above.

She grinned. "Don't need one. Take my hand."

He did, feeling that same spark of contact, and she led him, nimble and sure-footed as a mountain goat, through the grotto. Even in the dark, the white walls and spires seemed to faintly glow, as if lit from within. Soon, they emerged into the moonlight. The wind was fresh with the scent of warm earth and pine as they crossed the creek bed and scrabbled up the cliffside. The way home was clearly imprinted in Jo's mind; she moved with ease despite the dark, the rough terrain, and the heavy, damp fabric. All Owen could do was hold her hand and try to keep up.

When they reached her front door, he hesitated. In Fraser Springs, every window seemed to have a curious face peering out of it. He wanted badly to grab her by the waist, pull her hard against him, and kiss her in front of every last pair of prying eyes. With the meeting tomorrow, unfortunately, he knew better than to risk it.

Jo seemed to have the same thought. She had dropped his hand and was clearly trying to suppress a smile. "The path is just over there. You simply turned left when you should have turned right."

He gave her what he hoped was a solemn expression. "Thank you, ma'am. I don't know what I would have done if you hadn't found me."

"You'd probably still be wandering out there." Her lips quirked into a smile. "And there are wolves up in the hills."

He feigned a look of shock. "Why, I could have been torn to shreds." He dipped into a bow. "Thank you for your ... assistance."

Even in the dark, he could see the genuine smile spreading across her face. "The pleasure was all mine."

Chapter 18

The town of Fraser Springs was unnaturally still on the morning of the meeting. The wind had quieted, leaving an oppressive mugginess. Even the birds were silent, the way they were before a storm. The droning mosquitos seemed to be the only living things for miles.

At breakfast, Wilson's patrons sat in a quiet tableau, occasionally glancing at the boarded-up window as if expecting something to come bursting through. Humidity slicked the walls and fogged the glasses. Jo could barely stomach a bite of bread. Doc Stryker had come over for the morning meal, but even he picked at the edges of his bacon and stared off at nothing.

Around 10:00 a.m., the sound of hammering and sawing echoed off the buildings and the water.

"They're building a platform," said Nils, who had just arrived. "Right there by the wharf. Miss Jo, I think they plan to escort you out on the next boat."

"Stop that negative talk," she said, mustering up a confidence she didn't feel. "No one's hanging anyone; no one's hustling anyone out on the next boat. This isn't the Wild West."

"Surprised they aren't preparing the tar and feathers, the way they're carrying on," Doc snorted. "This is the most fun they've had all year."

Owen had promised to join them at the meeting, saying that he didn't want to look partial to her. As silly as it was, she wished he were beside her right now. She couldn't handle all these dour faces and their grim predictions. At least Owen would have been able to coax a smile out of her.

Soon, however, it was time to go. Ilsa and the girls had put on their church clothes and taken pains to give each other the most conservative hairstyles they knew. A few wore thin gold chains with crosses or heirloom brooches several decades old. It was strange to see her girls dressed as spinster schoolmarms, and Jo was touched by the gesture.

In the promenade by the wharf, the townspeople had constructed a raised platform decorated with bunting. A table flanked by four chairs—one for her, one for Doc Stryker, and two, she guessed, for the Society Ladies—stood on the platform along with a podium. The townspeople were well dressed and already flushed with anticipation, creating an almost festive atmosphere. Many of the women wore sashes decorated with needlepoint designating them as members of the Moral Purity Brigade, The Society for the Advancement of Moral Temperance, or the Ladies' Charitable Club. Jo half expected a brass band to begin playing and someone to hand her a glass of lemonade.

And in the middle of it all was Mrs. McSheen. She was flanked by her sash-wearing army of Society Ladies and positively glowed, despite the clouds and the mosquitos. Jo didn't think she had ever seen Mrs. McSheen smile, but today, the queen of the scowlers looked as if she'd won a beauty pageant. Moral crusading must be good for her skin.

She scanned the scene for Owen and found him leaning against the side of a building just outside of the crowd's perimeter. When he saw her, he gave her a reassuring nod, then pulled the brim of his hat down to obscure his expression. Still, she felt him looking at her as she made her way through the crowd, Doc Stryker by her side.

Right before they reached the platform, Doc grabbed her hand and squeezed it.

"You need to sacrifice me to save yourself, you just go ahead and do it," he whispered fiercely to her. "You just tell them that Old Doc Stryker put the idea of hiring women attendants in your head, brainwashed you. But now you see I'm a polluting influence and you're ready to become a proper Society Lady."

She squeezed his hand in return. "You know I wouldn't last a day as a Society Lady."

Doc chortled, despite the circumstances. He reached over and tucked behind her ear a rogue curl that had once again come loose from Jo's bun. "Maybe so, my dear. You've never even managed to put your hair up so it stays. Don't know how you'd ever make yourself one of those fancy sashes."

Mrs. McSheen made her way over with her entourage. The smile had been replaced with a world-class smirk. "Are you ready to begin?"

Jo flashed what she hoped was a dazzling smile. "Absolutely." She climbed the makeshift steps of the platform and took her place at the table. Nearly the entire town had turned out for the meeting: many people she recognized, and a few she didn't. The last time she'd seen the town gathered in these numbers was for Albert's funeral. That day had been humid too. The church had smelled of chrysanthemums and wet wool. As she'd stood up to address the crowd, her tears had blurred their faces into a smear of black and cream.

She took a breath. No tears today, only steely resolve. Like Owen, the loggers and miners hung at the perimeter of the gathering, unsure whether they counted as proper townspeople but wanting to support Jo. She tried hard to avoid staring at Owen, but she couldn't help it. Well, what did they say about being nervous when speaking in public? Imagine the crowd in their undergarments. So, fine, she was focusing on the one person she didn't have to try too hard to imagine undressed.

Her thoughts were interrupted by the general store clerk who had taken the podium. "I'd like to call the first official meeting of

Fraser Springs to order. As the temporarily designated mayor of Fraser Springs ..." A murmur shot through the crowd. There had been no mayoral elections. The clerk raised his voice and pressed on with his speech. "*As mayor*, I would like to welcome you to this gathering and remind you of our purpose." He was a little man, but he seemed to have grown half a foot with the prestige of his new position. His moustache gleamed with self-importance. "We are here, ladies and gentlemen, because our town is at a crossroads. We started as a rough-hewn mining town bestowed with the gift of the healing springs. Over the years, however, our town has grown. We have nurtured nature's bounty into a thriving tourist destination that now boasts one of the finest hotels west of the Rockies, and we're all immensely proud of the good work this community has accomplished."

A cheer went up from the townspeople. Everyone looked at the St. Alice, whose facade glimmered dully in the overcast light.

"But today, we have a decision to make. Do we want our town to retain the vestiges of its sinful past, or do we want to steer it towards a purer future?"

"Excuse me," Jo said. "But my understanding is that this is a town meeting, not a courtroom."

Another murmur from the crowd. The clerk frowned behind his perfect moustache.

"Ma'am, you'll have your chance to speak. But, yes, the decisions of this tribunal will not be binding, though it is worth noting that out here, the will of the people is all we have. We can't always do everything the way it's done in Vancouver or Victoria. We've got to stick together."

At this, there was a confident cheer. "Amen," someone exclaimed. As if on cue, the SS *Minto* glided into view, its paddle wheel churning. Maybe Nils was right. The paddle wheeler was not due back in dock until Tuesday. They were looking to run them out of town.

"Now, with that, we'd like to give Mrs. Josephine Wilson and Mr. Stryker ..."

"*Doctor* Stryker!" someone shouted, followed by a low ripple of laughter.

"Excuse me, *Doctor* Stryker, a chance to speak in their own defense. *Doctor* Stryker, would you like to go first?"

Doc stood and made his way to the podium. He looked almost frail, but determination radiated from him: an old, rangy dog with some fight still left. "I'm not one for speeches," he said finally. His voice revealed his false modesty. It was strong and clear, projecting over the crowd with the confidence of an experienced actor. "I prefer to save my pontificating and sermonizing for behind the counter of my establishment, if you know what I mean." Several townsmen chuckled despite themselves. "But I will say this. I've been in this town a long time. I've known some of you since you were small. I have had the privilege of hearing your troubles, counseling you on your problems, toasting your successes, and offering you comradery when I knew you were in a bad way.

"Not every problem, ladies and gentlemen, is fit for a pastor. Sometimes you need a stiff drink and the fellowship of your peers. You take away the one saloon in this town, and you'll take away a bit of the heart of this community. You all know that my establishment is in keeping with the spirit of the law, and if you're honest, you'll admit that it's within moral bounds as well. That's why there's a saloon like mine in every community from here up to the Arctic Circle and right down to Cape Horn. Probably it's the same clear around the world.

"Now, I'm an old man, and I'm an easy target to run out of here, but even the animals in the African savannah know the importance of a watering hole as a gathering place. You run me out, and you'll find two more saloons in my place. Ladies and gentlemen, I'd just like to say thank you to the community for over thirty years of business. Nearly every last one of you gentlemen has been in my saloon, and I've never judged any of you. Now, I'd kindly ask that you repay the favour."

Most of the men clapped, and the miners and loggers hooted and hollered. Doc Stryker gave them a thin smile as he made his way back to his seat. Mrs. McSheen's scowl had returned in full force.

It was Jo's turn. As she rose from her seat, her stomach clenched and she could hardly hear anything except the pounding of her heart. Placing her hands on either side of the podium, she took a deep breath and forced herself to look out over the crowd. "Always look like you know exactly what you're doing," Albert used to tell her. "If you *act* in charge, most people are happy to let you run things." She saw Ilsa and her girls, holding each other's hands in a chain of white-knuckled support. She saw Nils and her regulars, ready to shout down the first person who offered her the slightest disrespect. She saw Owen, the man who thought she was beautiful and brilliant and desirable. And she saw Mrs. McSheen, smirking again as if she'd already won. Jo squared her shoulders. If Mrs. McSheen wanted a fight, she would get it.

"Five years ago, my father and I sold the last of our possessions and arrived in Fraser Springs. We had been told there was medicine in the waters that might cure my father of his cough. But though my father could not be saved ..." She faltered, then recovered herself. "Though my father could not be saved, the care and compassion provided by the bathhouse attendants and by the people of Fraser Springs won my loyalty. It wasn't long before I married Albert Wilson."

"You seduced him!" someone cried out.

There was a brief, shocked silence. It was one thing to gossip but quite another to accuse a woman to her face, publicly, of being unchaste. Muttering—both approving and appalled—started up as Doc surged from his chair. Jo gave a small shake of her head, and he grudgingly returned to his seat. She'd expected this.

"I would ask you not to dishonour my late husband's memory," she said calmly. The crowd quieted more quickly than she'd expected. "You know that he was a savvy businessman and had a keen mind right up until the end. Our marriage was a comfort and a blessing to us both. Albert knew the value of that.

"When my father was sick, I saw what care the bathhouse attendants provided. Maybe that's why I decided to keep Wilson's Bathhouse going. I'm proud of the fact that my bathhouse is able to alleviate pain and suffering, and I'm proud that the women who work at my establishment are among the best trained and most virtuous in the country. That's the truth."

Her employees cheered, but she quieted them with a glance. "What's also the truth is that you know that these charges are unfounded. Many of you have been to my bathhouse or sat at my table. You know my staff. You know what goes on at Wilson's Bathhouse, and you know that none of it is obscene. It saddens me that you have felt it easier to go along with an exciting story than to admit the simple fact that my bathhouse is a part of this community, no matter whether the attendants are men, women, or trained chimpanzees."

The crowd was so still they seemed like a painted tableau. "I am not going anywhere, because I have done nothing wrong. I have tried my best to honour my husband's memory and carry on his life's work. If you have any proof of my wrongdoing, I hope you will present it so that I can refute it as the nonsense it is. If there is to be a vote, may you all vote according to your conscience."

Jo returned to her place at the table along with Doc, who shot her an approving glance. The miners and loggers, not to mention her girls, were cheering. The townspeople looked nervously at each other.

The clerk returned to the podium. "Mrs. McSheen, I believe you have a witness you would like to call."

Mrs. McSheen made her way to the podium. Her glow of self-satisfaction had returned. With her bustled skirt and frothy lace collar, she looked like an opera diva about to bring down the house with an aria.

"I'd like to thank you all for coming out," she said with her most gracious hostess voice. The townspeople clapped politely. "It means so very much to me, as it does for all the members of the Society for the Advancement of Moral Temperance." More clapping.

"Proverbs 28:13 says, 'He who conceals his transgressions will not prosper, but he who confesses and forsakes them will find compassion.' That is our mission today: compassion. Compassion for those who have sinned. But in order for God's purity and love to find its way to the hearts of Doctor Stryker and Mrs. Wilson, there needs to be confession. Make no mistake about it, ladies and gentlemen. The transgressions within their walls are all too real. Ephesians 5:11 cautions us, 'Do not participate in the unfruitful deeds of darkness, but instead expose them.'

"In that spirit, I would like to call Mr. Rusty Barlow up to the platform to share his testimony. Rusty ventured into Wilson's Bathhouse, and the story he has to tell is truly shocking. I will tell you in advance that this tale may not be suitable for children or women with more delicate sensibilities."

A hunched, rail-thin miner made his way up to the stage. Rusty had indeed been a customer. One of her least favourite, in fact. He was a brittle, malingering man who had once asked her to turn down the heat of the hot springs. As he climbed up onto the stage, he never looked up from his boots. He had shaved his beard and slicked back his hair, and someone had given him a clean suit to wear so that he looked almost respectable. He grasped the edges of the podium and blinked mole-like at his audience.

"Aww, I don't like being made a spectacle, but Mrs. McSheen asked me to share what I'd seen in Wilson's House of Sin." The other miners and loggers began to boo him.

"Shut up, Rusty, you ain't seen nothing!" one called.

"You old liar!" called another.

"If the gentlemen in the back cannot control their outbursts, they will be asked to leave," the "mayor" shouted. "Continue, Mr. Barlow."

Rusty avoided the crowd's gaze and continued staring at the ground. "Yes. Thank you. I can hardly tell my tale without shocking good Christian folk, but it needs to be said. I did venture to that there den of sin, and it's a hunnerd times worse than you can even imagine. The women of Wilson's offered themselves to me, and when I told them no, that I was a good Christian, they became enraged and insulted my manhood. When I called them vile creatures and prayed to God for strength, they hissed like snakes and began speakin' in tongues and running their claws over my skin, trying to tear at my flesh." He raised his gaze to the crowd. "It was then I knew the devil danced at Wilson's Bathhouse and them strumpets were his handmaidens. I ran out of there, and when I looked back, I saw them entangled in one another like a nest of vipers, men and women all engaged in the filthiest, carnal display."

Far from fainting, the good people of Fraser Springs hung on every word. Sensing his audience was captivated, Rusty lowered his voice again. "When I left, I made the sign of the cross, and I heard the devil laughing and his hooves clacking all around me as he danced. I had myself baptized that very day, and now I love the Lord." He looked at Mrs. McSheen. "And that's my story."

A din erupted as Rusty ceded the podium to the exceptionally smug "mayor."

"He's making it up!" Jo cried, but her voice was lost in the crowd.

The mayor called for silence, unsuccessfully. The only thing that quieted the crowd was a figure bounding up the steps of the stage two at a time: Owen Sterling. Jo cringed. He could only make this worse.

"I'd like to speak," Owen said as he climbed the platform. He did not look at her.

"My name is Ross Wister, and I'm a journalist." The crowd murmured. "I'm an outsider sent to Fraser Springs to find out the truth of what's going on at Wilson's Bathhouse, so the way I see it, my testimony should be welcome here."

The clerk nodded.

"Thank you," Owen said. "Ladies and gentlemen, a few weeks ago, I received a tip that young women were being held against their will at Wilson's and forced into a life of sin. I said to myself, 'Here's a story that the reading public needs to hear about. We need to do something to save these girls!' So I traveled up here, and do you know what I found?" He paused for dramatic effect. "A whole pack of nothing. I found hard-working young women using the healing waters of the hot springs to soothe the aches and pains of the community."

He gave a wry smile, acknowledging the scattered applause. "No one's more disappointed than I am, folks. My big story was nothing but rumours. Can't say it was the worst assignment I've ever had, since I enjoyed a good night's sleep in the St. Alice and some excellent treatments at Wilson's, but I can assure you—"

"What else did you enjoy at Wilson's?" came a cry.

"He's in with that woman! I saw 'em walking alone last night!" came another.

"Tainted!" Mrs. McSheen cried. "He's in her clutches!"

"I did not fall into anyone's clutches," Owen said. Remarkably, he did not even so much as blush. "And I don't care what you busybodies think you saw. You all seem to keep such good tabs on the people of this town, I'm interested in how none of you overheard great masses of men and women entangled in sin as the devil tap danced. How did all you hundreds of people living not a few feet away from one another miss that, when I can't so much as speak to Mrs. Wilson without a dozen people whispering about it? I bet you know exactly what your neighbour had for breakfast, what kind of laundry soap she uses. There are no secrets in towns like these."

Owen leaned forward at the podium, completely comfortable in his role as a speaker. "What a town like this does have, however, is rumour. Rumour breeds quicker than these mosquitos. It's more contagious than a plague and can lead to as much destruction."

He smiled grimly at Mrs. McSheen. "Ladies and gentlemen, I am a stranger who has spent less than a week in your town, but it is clear that you are good, moral people trying to do the right thing. It seems, however, that you have let rumour and gossip get the best of you, and it's causing your minds to invent feverish plots. You've got this paddle wheeler ready to run two good people out of town based upon on the ramblings of an old, demented miner! No, I believe that you are all better than that. Drop this witch hunt and return these businesspeople to their place in your community. I am calling on you to do the right thing."

A great hush had fallen. Even the lapping of the waves against the wharf seemed to have ceased.

As casual as could be, he adjusted a cufflink and smiled at the crowd. "Well, ladies and gentlemen, there's another thing you haven't considered." The townspeople stopped. Mrs. McSheen looked nervously at her cronies. "As I said, I am a journalist. And right now, I am a journalist without a story, which is not such a great position to be in. But, lucky for me, my readers like a good scandal. All this drama, these mysterious bricks through windows, the threatening letters? You've got some real front page material here.

"Now, I like this town. I like you, the people of this town. This is a place the whole world should see. But as a man of the fifth estate, I have a sworn duty to tell the truth, no matter how much that truth may impact the local tourist economy. So you all act according to your consciences, but just remember that you probably shouldn't do anything you wouldn't be proud to read about on the front page of the morning paper."

The townspeople had stilled again. All of them were looking at Mrs. McSheen and the new "mayor," both of whom glanced uncertainly at one another.

"Anyone want to step up to be quoted in the paper on this matter? Mr. Mayor, perhaps I could get a few words from you on the subject," Owen said. The mayor and McSheen looked furious but kept their peace. "No? Well, it seems like that's settled."

He clapped his hands in boyish delight. "Now, since this day already seems so festive with the bunting and the sashes, what say we retreat from this terrible humidity to the parlour of the St. Alice for its world-class tea service?"

To Jo's great surprise, the people at the edges of the crowd began to break away. A few even started to head in the direction of the hotel. No one jeered or tried to shout Owen down. It felt as if all the meeting's anger had suddenly dissipated into awkward embarrassment.

The mayor rushed to the stand, shouldering Owen aside. "Ladies and gentlemen, we've not yet finished! There's still much to discuss." But the tide had turned, and the crowd continued to disperse. In truth, she doubted that many of them had wanted either of the establishments gone in the first place. Owen had provided them with a way to save face. Later, they could say that they were only thinking of the town's reputation.

Owen had leapt down from the stage and was merrily trotting along beside the townspeople, opening the door to usher them into the St. Alice. Soon, the square was empty save for her girls, women in sashes, and the red-faced mayor, whose moustache quivered like a compass needle. Doc took her arm.

"Shall we, young lady?" he asked.

Jo smiled. Together, they stepped off the platform where Nils and the girls clamoured around them. Between the soupy air and the sudden turn of events, she felt as if she were walking through a dream. The SS *Minto* bobbed idly at the dock—yes, the stakes really had been that high.

The girls' words blended together into wordless chatter, like a flock of starlings. Her head swam. She was grateful for Owen's intervention, but what would happen after he left? Because he would surely leave, wouldn't he?

She didn't want to think about it. The problem had been sorted for now. Maybe the townspeople had indeed come to their senses.

"Drinks are on me," Doc said, and they all followed him away. She couldn't hold back a little smile as they passed Mrs. McSheen, still standing with her cronies on the platform, their sashes hanging limp in the warm, damp air.

Chapter 19

Inside the St. Alice, Owen heartily shook hands and dispensed compliments on Fraser Springs's good sense and commitment to justice. He even praised the dry scones, though the raisins in them reminded him of fossilized creatures trapped in shale. He once again waxed poetic on the virtues of the hot springs and the pure air and the wilderness, and assured the good people of Fraser Springs that his readers would surely flock to this place.

After half an hour, the mayor, Mrs. McSheen, and her fellow sash-wearers joined the party. Mrs. McSheen approached him with a smile that did not extend to her eyes. Her hands were clenched at her sides.

"So you're a journalist!" she said, with a gaiety that had a manic edge. "Well, fancy the thought. I do hope you'll be telling your readers about the many health benefits of our springs."

"Of course, madam," he assured her. "Even though I would love to keep this hidden gem for myself, it's my journalistic duty to inform the world about the treasures you have here." The treacly words felt hollow as he spoke them.

"Very good, very good," she said. She lifted her chin a few degrees higher and looked evenly at him. The painted-on smile disappeared. "After all, it's no good to keep secrets, now is it?"

With this, she retreated into the crowd, where she stood in a tight knot with several of the ladies and the mayor. Owen wanted desperately to go to Jo. She had been magnificent this afternoon, staring down her accusers from atop that silly platform. Like a modern-day Joan of Arc. He'd never wanted to kiss a woman more. Still, he knew that even being seen with her would ruin all of his hard work. They'd almost been caught once already. No, it was important to have patience. He would see her soon enough.

And so he listened while the mayor chattered on about the plans for increasing the SS *Minto*'s runs to allow for more tourist traffic, and he choked down another scone, though he felt that he was eating the stuffing of the plush wing-backed chairs in the lobby, and he praised an old woman on her very fine sash and heard about all the good works she'd done to earn it.

Soon, however, the townspeople filtered out to attend to their suppers. The usual bustle had been restored to Fraser Springs. It seemed that the good citizens had gotten it all out of their system. Even Mrs. McSheen and her band of malcontents seemed resigned.

Just as Owen was about to leave, the spotty young man who worked at the general store approached him.

"You sure knocked some sense into these folks," he said.

"I was just trying to provide an outsider's view," Owen said. "Sometimes when you live in a place, it can be hard to see the forest for the trees."

"Sure are a lot of trees here," the boy said.

"Yes, indeed. I know I certainly got swept up with the story when I first came here, but cooler heads have prevailed."

The boy gave him a wary look. "I hope so. But I know these folks, and I can't say I've ever seen them let things blow over so quickly."

Owen gave him what he hoped was a fatherly look. "I know so," he said.

As they walked into the hall, he saw Mrs. McSheen conversing with a few women in sashes, the mayor, and Rusty. Rusty was especially animated. As Owen passed by, however, they quieted. He couldn't get close enough to understand what they were saying.

"Nice to meet you," he made a point of saying loudly to the boy as they parted ways. "Now I'm off to write a nice, long article about this place."

And with that, he retreated to his room. He shed his suit jacket, removed his tie and collar, and unbuttoned the first buttons on his shirt. Give it another hour, and then he could head over to Wilson's under the cover of getting supper. He sat down at the room's little table and looked out over Fraser Springs. The town was awash in a cloudy, jaundiced glow from the sun trying its best to fight through the humidity and the clouds. He could hear the mosquitos droning even through the glass.

Constitutions restored in miracle town! he wrote, then crossed it out.

Forget the big city vacation and explore this great province's health-restoring bounty!

No, that sounded too much like an advertisement.

Feisty young businesswoman has health-restoring charms. Small-town drama worth it for another taste of those lips, journalist reports.
Let the cares of the city slip away in a wild paradise. Doctors agree that hot springs have very real restorative properties.

He tried to distract himself with the list of experts he would have to consult to give this piece a little heft when he returned home.

When he returned home. He'd been so caught up in the drama of the story and the charms of Jo Wilson that the idea of returning home had completely slipped his mind. Staying in Fraser Springs was, of course, out of the question. He had his own life to get back to: his club, his writing, his speaking engagements, his editor, the little circuit of pubs and restaurants where the waiters all knew him.

And surely after all this unpleasantness, she wouldn't seriously want to stay in Fraser Springs. After the article came out, she could find a buyer who could pay a handsome price for her establishment. She could move down to Vancouver. He'd give up his bachelor apartment, and they'd settle in together in a little suite somewhere downtown. And when his journalistic career took off, they could move to one of those grand homes in New Westminster with the wraparound porches and the well-kept lawns. His friends would love her.

There was a lot to discuss and no time like the present. It was time for supper. He bounded down the stairs two at a time into the lobby. It was empty as a tomb and just as marble-clad. The last few malcontents had probably gone back home to lick their wounds and sullenly set supper out for their husbands. Good riddance. Jo didn't need to worry about them any longer. He would make sure of that.

• • •

It had been years since Jo had set foot in Doc Stryker's bar, but she would have recognized the scent of pipe smoke, sweat, and alcohol anywhere, even without the patrons. The odour seemed to have been cured into the wood. The light turned amber coloured as it passed through the tobacco-stained windows, making Jo feel that she was trapped in a sepia photograph. Still, the place was clean, and Doc had obviously taken immense pride in varnishing the long bar and shining the mirror that reflected the rows of bottles in front of it.

"Now I know this is no place for fine ladies such as yourselves, but pull up a chair, and I'll get us a celebratory round," he said.

Half of her girls were former barmaids, so they all felt right at home in the environment. They found seats and immediately began unpinning their church hairdos and shaking out their curls.

"I thought you was done for, Miz Jo," Ilsa said. "I almost started to cry. When that Rusty got up there, I thought that crowd was going to rip you to pieces."

"Should have popped Rusty in the nose when I had the chance," said another girl, miming the action. "He once tried to put his hand up my skirt, and when I told him off, he called me words I can't even repeat. Should have slapped his lying mouth right there and then."

"Wonder if Mrs. McSheen paid him for his little story," Nils said. "Although Rusty's so darned crazy, he likely believes all that nonsense."

Doc rummaged around behind the bar and came up with a dusty wine bottle. "Been saving this for a special occasion, and I can't think of a finer one than today," he said, running his thumb over the pattern embossed on the glass.

Everyone cheered. Doc lined up some tiny crystal glasses on the bar and poured the crowd a drink. While Jo had enjoyed the occasional glass of claret with Albert after dinner, since his death, her desire for drink had never been great enough for her to stomach the disapproving glare she would surely get from the clerk at the general store should she try to purchase a bottle.

She took a glass and raised it aloft.

"To justice!" Doc said.

"To justice!" they all chorused.

The wine tasted like molasses and raisins. A warm flush spread down her throat and across her chest. Jo let out a breath she didn't realize she was holding.

"You should have seen Mrs. McSheen's face when Mr. Wister was speaking." Ilsa giggled. "She looked like she could lunge across the table and strangle him with her gloves."

"And that don't compare to Rusty's face. Those crazy eyes almost popped out of his head and rolled across the floor," Nils said.

Jo sat back and listened to her employees' happy chatter. They were street-smart women, and if they weren't worried, why should she be? Best to relax and enjoy the victory, no matter how short-lived she feared it might be. Doc Stryker found another bottle of wine, and the group once again toasted to their health, to the prosperity of their businesses, and to "Ross Wister." Where was Owen? The flush from the wine spread across her body.

Soon, however, it was time for the girls to get back to the serious business of mealtimes at Wilson's. Nils excused himself on some errand or other, leaving Doc and Jo alone in the bar. Doc motioned for her to come sit on the stools at the counter. He brought out his jug of hooch.

"Oh, I can't," she protested. "I've got to be presentable for dinner service."

Doc smiled. "Suit yourself." He poured himself a drink but did not raise it to his lips.

"Now listen," he said. "There's something I been meaning to talk to you about. This journalist fellow."

Hopefully, the wine flush hid her blush. "What about him?" she asked.

Doc smiled. "Ain't no need to be ashamed. I seen him and I seen you, and I know how people act when they're sweet on each other." He grinned and tapped a finger to his temple. "Old Doc Stryker's got that power of observation. Nah, the two of you: it's a fine match. You know I think of you like a daughter, and I would be proud to have any daughter of mine marry that man. Lord knows he's terrible at keeping a low profile, but he's got a good head on his shoulders and a kind heart. It's been a lot of hard years for you, Jo. You deserve some happiness."

She didn't know what to say, but the old man was not done. He stared beyond her, then down into the murky liquid in his glass. "I don't know if I ever told you that I was married once. Years ago. Had two little ones, too. Two girls. And one day cholera came through and ..." He swept his hand in a dismissive motion, unable to say the words.

"I was young then, and I always said I would remarry when the time was right. When I had money to pay for real doctors to treat my family if they got sick or to buy 'em a nice house with a yard, you know. I met my share of eligible women but always found some fault in them or in the timing or in the circumstances. Maybe after the summer carnival season. Maybe when I get the bar up and running. Maybe when I'm thirty or when I'm forty.

"But the truth is, it's hard to open yourself up to someone new after you seen the three people you love best looking like wax dolls all laid out on a table, after you paid the last of your money to build a coffin big enough so all three of 'em could be together 'cause you couldn't bear to put those little girls in the ground alone. I knew, deep down, that I just couldn't do it again." The old man's eyes were bright, and his voice quavered.

"And I always regretted it. I don't want to see you fending off bankruptcy and mean-spirited gossip for the rest of your life. You deserve better than that."

"But it's not about what I deserve," Jo objected. "I have my girls to think about."

Doc shrugged. "Your girls are grown women, not babies you've got to lead on your apron strings. And they're all scrappers, bless 'em. They'll muddle through." He reached over the bar and took her hand. "You're young yet, girl. You should have babies of your own."

Jo's throat clenched. She'd wanted that desperately during her time with Albert, and it had never happened for them. She remembered the day after Albert's funeral when she'd curled up on his side of the bed just to smell his hair tonic on the pillow. She had been overwhelmed by the weight of how utterly alone she was and had resolved to never feel that vulnerable again. In truth, though, being with Owen was the first time she'd relaxed in five years. That hand on her waist, that hollow by his throat where she'd rested her head ...

"So say I move to Vancouver and it doesn't work out. If a man can fall in love in a few days, he can fall out of love just as fast, and what then? I'd be back to where I started, with no friends, no family, and not a penny in the bank."

Jo blinked back the sudden heat of tears, hoping that Doc didn't notice. How had she come apart so quickly? Before Owen showed up, she would have never let anyone see her cry.

Doc touched her shoulder. "No one's saying to sell up right this minute. But if there's anything I've learned, it's that it's no good arranging your life just to avoid pain. Pain will find you anyhow, so you might as well go after what you want." He picked up a glass and started to polish it. "Ah, what am I doing giving you advice? You're a thousand times smarter than I am."

What had seemed like common sense now felt like cowardice. Was she really planning on shutting herself away in her office forever? She'd tried that, and all it had gotten her was an angry crowd and a brick through her front window.

As if on cue, she heard the shatter of breaking glass. Something flew across the room and crashed into the mirror behind the bar.

"Get down!" Doc yelled. As Jo flung herself onto the floor, a hundred bottles of liquor went up in a deafening explosion of blue flame. Acrid smoke and tongues of fire billowed up to the ceiling, engulfed the wood of the bar, raced along the floor and up the wallpaper.

Coughing and half-blind, they stumbled and crawled towards the door. But no matter how fast they were, the fire was faster. She could no longer see the door for the choking smoke.

"Stay low," Doc shouted. "Cover your face!"

Her lungs burned with each panicked breath.

"Windows?" she gasped, just as the windows shattered from the heat of the blaze. Jo screamed.

The tar-black smoke was making it impossible to breathe. She and Doc crawled towards the back of the bar, which was the only place not ablaze. The curtains caught fire. The varnish was peeling off the chairs and tables and turning to ash before their eyes. Jo coughed uncontrollably, trying to remain low to the ground. Was there another exit? She couldn't remember. They huddled against the wall as the fire pressed down upon them.

Chapter 20

Owen was halfway to Wilson's when he heard a man ranting, followed by breaking glass. By the time he ran to Doc Stryker's bar, it was already awash in flames. A small, twisted figure danced by the inferno, still wearing his good suit. His dark eyes were bright with the reflection of the flames, and his hair was standing up wildly.

Rusty.

"You devils want some fire? Here's some fire for ye. Hope it chokes you right to hell." He laughed, waving his arms in a bizarre dance. "Fornicators and wicked women do love the devil, so they can go straight to hell to dance with him!"

"Jo's in there!" Nils shouted. The big man was barreling towards the bar at a dead run. "So's Doc Stryker." He lowered his shoulder and plowed into Rusty just before Owen could reach him. The two men rolled head over heels into the gravel.

Owen could feel the searing heat from yards away. The paint on the boardwalk bubbled. "Grab some buckets," he shouted at the crowd that was assembling.

Doc Stryker's entire facade was engulfed. There was no way in. Owen ran into Wilson's woodshed and grabbed the axe propped against the door. If he couldn't go through the front door, he would make his own.

Just then, he heard a scream from the back of the building. Doc's bar was built half on land and half on pilings driven into the water. Owen ran to the edge of the lake then shimmied his way up the post. Bits of burning ash and debris showered down on him.

Undeterred, he wrapped his legs around the top post and used his upper body to hoist himself, still carrying the axe, up onto the decking that supported the back half of the building.

The heat of the blaze nearly knocked him back, but he regained his footing and squinted through the smoke and the fumes rolling off the alcohol-soaked wood. Above him, something cracked, and he ducked just in time to miss a fiery beam crashing into the hot springs.

Owen heard another scream. "Jo! Doc! I'm coming!" he yelled. "Head towards my voice!"

The wind had picked up, and a tongue of fire jutted skyward. Underneath the fire's crackling, Owen heard splintering. The whole rickety structure was about to go down.

Owen heaved his axe and chopped at the back wall of the building. That didn't go fast enough, so he dropped the axe and kicked at the planks with all his strength. Finally, he made just enough of an opening in the splintered planks and ragged plaster to enter.

"Jo!" he yelled. "Doc!"

No answer. The smoke was so thick that he could only make out the hazy shapes. None of them seemed to be human.

"Jo!" He dropped to his knees and crawled farther into the blaze. His heart was thrumming and the smoke seared his nose and throat, but Owen felt strangely calm. He had a single purpose now, and he would rather die than fail at it. His entire existence had been narrowed down to this moment, to the single-minded search for the outline of a human shape. Jo was inside somewhere, and she needed him, and he *would* find her.

• • •

She could no longer hear the roar of the fire. Her ears were filled with the wheeze of her own breathing as she struggled for air.

Beside her, Doc slumped lifelessly. Someone called her name, but she couldn't be sure who it was. Her father or Albert, maybe, welcoming her home. She could vaguely make out their bodies as they came towards her in the smoke. A sense of peace filled her. They had come for her. They wouldn't let her die alone.

And suddenly, cool air. A voice. Someone was calling her name. She tried to cry out, but her voice was smothered by the smoke.

"Jo!" someone yelled. She could no longer remember where she was. Was she in the grotto? The walls did not feel smooth enough. Why was she so tired? With as much energy as she could muster, she forced herself to her knees and crawled towards the oxygen. And then someone grabbed her.

"Owen?" she croaked.

"We're getting you out of here," he said.

"Oh," she gasped. "Yes." And then, somehow, she was out in the open air.

"Are you hurt?" he asked her.

Her head was muddled, her ears ringing so that she could barely hear Owen's question. She tried to focus. "No," she said. "Get Doc!" It felt as if her throat were swelling shut. "Against the wall," she rasped. "At the back." Coughing racked her entire body and took away her ability to speak.

"Owen," she tried to say, but she was lifted off the platform away from the heat and into the arms of a dozen townspeople. Then the world swung crazily and went black. The next thing she knew, a female voice was repeating, "It's okay, it's okay, we've got you." Through her soot-crusted eyes, she tried to peer at the scene in front of her. What was the SS *Minto* doing at Doc's? And where was Owen? Why couldn't she stop coughing?

Jo knew she must be hallucinating, because Mrs. McSheen was kneeling over her, wiping her eyes and mouth with a lacy handkerchief. "It's going to be okay." And that was when she fainted again.

Chapter 21

When his hand found Jo's boot through the smoke, Owen's body coursed with relief and adrenaline. It was all he could do to not stop where they were and kiss her. As he lifted her into his arms and began staggering to the hole in the back wall, he wondered how he could get her to safety. She was practically unconscious, obviously too weak to climb or swim far.

He burst free into the sunlight.

"Are you hurt?" Owen asked Jo as he gasped for breath.

She shook her head. "No. Get Doc!" She began coughing and gestured vaguely towards the direction she'd come from. "Against the wall," she managed. "At the back."

The SS *Minto* had braved the flames and almost run itself aground to get close to the burning structure and offer assistance. Men with buckets tried to douse the blaze, though it seemed clear that the building was a complete loss. Owen swung Jo over the railing into the arms of six men waiting on the boat, took a gulp of good air, and headed back into the inferno. On the boat, people shouted for him to not be stupid. "I have to get Doc!" he shouted back. He wouldn't let Jo down.

The interior of the bar was black with smoke. Owen dropped again to his knees and crawled in the direction Jo had told him. Doc was there, curled on his side with his face buried in his arms.

"Doc!" He tried to shake the man awake, but he didn't move.

Using the dregs of the strength left in his body, Owen grabbed both of Doc's arms and dragged him towards safety.... *Don't die, don't die, don't die.*

With a last burst of desperate energy, he pulled Doc through the hole in the wall and out into the daylight. It took several people to get Doc's limp body over the railing and onto the deck. Owen hopped over after him, and the SS *Minto* began churning away towards the center of the lake. Moments later, the fire must have reached Doc's carefully hidden still, because the fire surged with a roar. The explosion was enough to send the whole structure toppling sideways into the water.

He knelt by Doc Stryker's body. The old man's face was grey, his lips blue beneath a film of black soot. Still, his pulse fluttered faintly beneath Owen's fingertips. The man was alive but barely. He wiped the crusted soot from Doc's nose and mouth.

"We need to flip him over," he called, and a few men helped to roll Doc over onto his stomach so that his head was resting on Owen's knees.

Owen began compressing Doc's chest, then raising the man's elbows up and down to open his lungs. "Out with the bad air, in with the good air," he mumbled. "Out with the bad air, in with the good air."

Doc didn't stir.

"Come on, old man!" He kept trying, imagining that Doc's arms were bellows stoking the breath back into his lungs.

"You're too tough to go this way. Come on."

Finally, the old man gasped raggedly. Owen rolled him over onto his back. Slowly, his eyes fluttered open and colour came back into his cheeks. He coughed and spat black soot on to the deck, then gulped for air.

"Thank God," Owen murmured.

Doc's hair was singed, and his lips were parched. Someone brought him a glass of water.

"You gave us a scare, Doc," Owen said.

Doc coughed several times and spat up more black phlegm. "Takes more ... than fire ... to ... kill me." He tried to smile. Suddenly, panic flashed across his face.

"She's fine," Owen assured him. "Got her out before you." Owen looked over to where Jo was sitting, propped against the railing. Maybe it was because he had almost lost her, but even though her face was streaked with soot and her hair was falling down, she looked more beautiful than ever.

She saw him looking at her and smiled wanly. He left Doc's side and sat down beside her, resting his hand against hers. It felt natural, as if their hands had many years of practice resting beside one another.

"Well, that's about all the excitement I can take for today," he said. "What about you?"

She laughed weakly. From a distance, he could see that the whole town had a bucket brigade out and was digging a wide firebreak through the stretch of brush between the inferno of Doc's bar and the dry timbers of Wilson's. Funny how the people who wanted to send Jo packing were now, mere hours later, putting out the fire that threatened to burn Wilson's to the ground.

"Looks like they're saving your business," he said.

"Well, that's a change." She brushed her thumb against his wrist. He gave her hand a squeeze. With his free hand, he brushed a fleck of ash from her cheek.

"There," he said. "That's better."

• • •

With Owen beside her and the fire reflecting brilliantly off the gentle ripples of the lake, Jo felt almost peaceful. The waves lapped against the boat in a gentle cadence that threatened to lull her into sleep. It was the lingering effects of the smoke inhalation, she suspected. Everything moved at such a dream-like pace, maybe she had, in fact, perished in the fire.

Strangest of all was Mrs. McSheen, who seemed to have traded her crusade against Jo for a new career as a quartermaster. As the boat docked, Mrs. McSheen bustled off to direct the ladies' efforts in a hundred helpful directions.

"Lucy, be a dear and run back to my house and cut the cake that's on the counter into pieces, then wrap the slices in waxed paper. Maude, take Ann and get the big coffee urn from the church basement and the coffee from the tin next to it. And while you're there, ask the reverend what the meeting hall's availability is. It's going to take a lot of fundraising to set this right, and there's no time to waste."

Even without her management, the firefighting efforts were being conducted with remarkable efficiency and even good cheer. A bucket brigade was throwing water on the last stubborn embers of Doc's bar. Another group of men shoveled dirt and sand onto the wreckage. Ilsa and the rest of Jo's girls had turned the bathhouse kitchen into a dinner assembly line, churning out ham sandwiches to feed all the volunteers.

All that was left of Doc Stryker's was the big pot-bellied stove, which stoically stood guard over the smoldering ruins. By some miracle, however, Wilson's Bathhouse suffered only smoke stains up the side of the facade and a few windows blown out from the heat.

Doc stood unsteadily on the gangplank, surveying the scene with smoke-reddened eyes. Everything he had built over the past thirty years had been reduced to smoke and ash. He was propped upright by two of his loyal patrons, one on either side.

"We'll rebuild it, Doc," Jo said. "We'll set it right."

He simply nodded, dazed. He hardly seemed to be listening.

She motioned to the two men. "Take him to my place and put him in the upstairs bedroom."

Somewhere down the boardwalk, a man suddenly began shouting, angry and wild. Two other figures tussled with him.

"What's going on?" she asked.

"Looks like Rusty lost his fool mind," said an old miner taking a rest from the bucket brigade. "Smashed in and lit the place on fire, ranting about perdition and the devil. They got him hog-tied, but he's still giving them fits." He scowled in Rusty's direction. "Let all of us deal with him, that's what I say, but that new mayor's gonna put him on the boat and send him to the RCMP down in Vancouver. He's already telegraphed into Nelson to get a constable to come deal with him on the boat ride over."

The miner spat on the ground. "Crazy old coot. Hope he rots in jail."

Seemingly out of nowhere, Ilsa ran up and threw her arms around Jo. "Oh, Miz Jo," she sobbed.

Jo rubbed the woman's back. "I'm fine, Ilsa. But Doc isn't. Can you get him cleaned up and make sure he has everything he needs?"

Ilsa brushed a tear away with the back of her thumb. "Right away, Miz Jo."

"Put Annie in charge of doling out the food."

"Yes, Miz Jo."

"And if you need more coffee, there should be four new tins in the pantry on the top shelf."

"Yes, Miz Jo."

"And cut it with chicory to stretch it. Perhaps set out the big basins for the men to wash up in?"

Ilsa put her hands on Jo's shoulders. "We've got it all sorted," she said, gently. "Now go get some rest."

"I just need to make sure that—"

Ilsa motioned Owen over. He'd been lingering around at the edge of the conversation, unwilling to leave Jo's side. "Miz Jo is simply not able to take a day off, even on days when she almost dies in a fire," she said. "Could you escort her upstairs and make sure that she stays in her bed?"

Owen smiled. "My pleasure," he said, taking Jo gently by the arm and leading her towards Wilson's.

"I'm not an invalid! I'm perfectly capable of—"

Owen just smiled at her. "You certainly are. But right now, your staff is even more capable. And you smell like a campfire. At least come inside and get cleaned up."

She couldn't help but return his smile. Together, they headed up the stairs.

Chapter 22

At the door to Jo's bedroom, Owen hesitated. There was no chapter in the *Manual of Proper Gentleman's Conduct* on what to do when a lady has just escaped from certain death in a burning building and a gentleman has been deputized to put her to bed. Jo gave him a tentative smile, then frowned at his arm.

"You're hurt," she said.

Now that she mentioned it, his arm was, indeed, throbbing. A ragged welt of burned skin blistered across his forearm. He shrugged. "I'm fine."

She took him by the hand and led him into her bedroom. "I'll take care of it."

"I'm fine," he repeated. "I don't even remember when it happened." Her bedroom smelled of her perfume and of lavender; the bed seemed to take up his entire field of vision, all soft quilts and embroidered pillowcases. He tore his eyes away from it with a determined effort.

Jo was already rummaging around in her vanity table drawer, and she quickly found whatever it was she was looking for. "You can run into a burning building, but you're scared of a little salve and a bandage?"

He grimaced as she pried the lid from a small tin. "I ran into a burning building *twice*, thank you. And I can smell that stuff from here. Bet it strips the flesh right off." The tin's contents smelled frighteningly medicinal—some strange combination of pine sap and cheap whiskey. Did all the cures in Fraser Springs involve alcohol?

"Sit," she ordered, gesturing to the little vanity stool.

Owen shook his head at her determination. "I have very clear orders to be taking care of you, not the other way round."

Jo didn't answer. Instead, she brought an enamel basin of water over from its stand near the room's single window, set it on the vanity, and glared at him expectantly. Resigned to his fate, he sat. Carefully, since the little stool seemed too dainty for actual use. She knelt beside him, wet a washcloth, wrung it out, and began gently daubing at the soot and blood covering his forearm. Clearly not a squeamish woman—no missish airs for Jo Wilson.

When the burn was cleaned to her satisfaction, she applied the salve. Even though her fingertips brushed his skin as tenderly as a caress, the stuff stung like hell. Just as he'd suspected. He tried not to wince, and at least she worked quickly. Jo wrapped his forearm with a strip of soft cotton and tucked in the ends.

"And we're done," she said. She ran her fingers from the edge of the bandage down to his wrist. Despite the pain in his arm, the lingering brush of her fingers sent a thrilling pulse through him. "That wasn't so bad now, was it?"

"Speak for yourself." Owen leaned over and took the washcloth from the basin, squeezing the water out with one hand. "You're a mess," he said tenderly, running the damp rag against her cheek. Was she smiling or grimacing? Her expression was difficult to read. Slowly, the cloth restored the creamy whiteness of her cheeks, her neck, her collarbone.

He placed the washcloth back in the basin and ran his hands over her hair, brushing away the clinging flecks of powdery ash. The motion released more of that mint and talc fragrance so native to her that even fire couldn't burn it out. He traced the curving edges of her ears with his thumbs, his fingers sweeping loosely along the nape of her lovely, pale neck.

But just as he leaned in to kiss her, her eyes were suddenly bright with welling tears.

"Aw, honey," he said and pulled her up to his lap, enfolding her in his arms. She collapsed against him, her head buried in his neck. "You're okay," he murmured into her hair. "I've got you. You're okay."

She sobbed against him, her ribs and shoulders heaving. She was so small, really. Her toughness made her seem much larger, like a cat puffing itself up in self-defense.

"You're okay," he repeated. And suddenly the enormity of what had happened swept over him as well. Swarming images of the fire, of Doc's slumped body, of Jo's hand reaching out through the smoke, caught his breath and clamped down around his throat. No more talking, then.

He rose and carried her the three short steps to her bed. She wrapped her arms around him and pressed her face into his shirt, clinging to him even after he laid her down and started to pull away from her.

"Stay, please?" she whispered. The raggedness of her voice wrecked him.

"Of course." He toed off his boots and stretched out alongside her. "For as long as you want, sweetheart."

Her weeping slowed to hiccuping gulps, but he didn't let her go. He stroked her neck, caressed the soft valley between her shoulders and down her back. "I've got you," he said, no longer entirely sure which of them he meant to comfort with the words. "You're okay. I've got you."

• • •

Her sleep was deep and dreamless.

She woke to a room barely illuminated by the thin light of dawn. Even in the dimness, Jo could see that the pillows and sheets were streaked with dirt and ash. She was wearing yesterday's clothes, now most likely irreparably wrinkled and stained, and a hairpin was jabbing into her scalp. Her eyes were still aching and gritty from weeping. How long had it been since she had cried in front of anyone? Since she had cried at all?

She moved her arm to remove the wretched little hairpin, and the back of her hand brushed against warm skin. Owen was still beside her in bed, warm and real and solid. The comfort of simple physical closeness felt decadent. She tried to keep her movements small and quiet as she untangled her skirts from around her legs. Owen shifted and slid his arm around her tightly. Jo smiled to herself and gave in to the urge to snuggle in closer.

She had forgotten about his blistered forearm. Owen jolted awake with a painfully drawn-in breath that made her wince away in sympathy.

"Oh! I'm so sorry."

Owen's eyes were open, but he seemed not to register where he was. He took a deep, shuddering breath. Her hand was still against his chest, and she could feel his heart pounding. Finally, he looked down at her and his expression softened.

He kissed the top of her head. She could feel his pulse slowing, the soft movement of his breath against her hair, his muscles relaxing beneath her.

"Don't be sorry," he said. "I wasn't enjoying my dreams." He sighed in and out deeply. "Everything still smells like fire."

She smoothed her fingers down his chest, tracing the streaks of soot on his shirt. "Did I remember to thank you for saving my life?" she whispered, smiling at him.

He managed a smile. "For you, anything. And for Doc Stryker too." He paused and again she felt the tension return to his body. "God, his face was so grey. I thought for sure ..."

For a long moment, they held each other in silence. She knew they were both replaying the scene from yesterday. Jo took a breath. If she thought too hard, she would start thinking of the narrowly avoided possible endings. "But we're all okay," she finally said.

"We're okay," he agreed. "Even if we're a mess," he whispered, smiling at her. His forehead was still faintly smudged with ash, and his fair hair and blue eyes stood out that much more brightly.

And that was when he kissed her, and all the possible endings vanished. There was just one ending—this one, the one that led to this bed with the dawn light creeping in the window and across her bright quilt. He threaded his fingers through her hair, and somehow despite the tangles his hand found its way down to her shoulders. His lips followed, kissing along her neck to the hollow at her throat.

He pushed her down gently into the pillows and slipped one arm beneath her waist to pull her even more tightly to him. Instinctively, she arched her back and closed her eyes as her breasts pressed against the unyielding wall of his chest, and he kissed her again deeply. His blond stubble scratched against her chin, and she didn't care.

They were still both fully clothed, but Owen's shirttails had pulled loose from his trousers, and her roaming fingers soon strayed over the bare skin of his back, his sides, his shoulders. She brushed her fingernails down his spine and reveled in the shivering response. The fabric of her own clothing felt rough against the hard peaks of her nipples, and her legs felt bound by her skirts. As if he were responding to her own sensations, Owen reached down with one hand and roughly pulled her skirts and petticoat up around her thighs.

She exhaled sharply as he pulled her newly freed right leg over his hip, bringing the ache between her legs against his unmistakable hardness. She tilted her hips ever so slightly, exploring the sensation. Almost immediately, he tore his lips away from hers and buried his face in the curve of her neck, and his heavy breath chased maddeningly across the sensitive skin there. His free hand came to her hip.

"God, Jo," he ground out. "Jo. Tell me what you want."

She had no idea what she wanted. Gorgeous sensations had erased every coherent thought from her head. She wound her leg more tightly around him, and felt as much as heard Owen stifle a moan. The sound made her brave, shameless. She ran her hand down his back, letting it linger over the tight planes of his waist and his buttocks.

"I want you inside me," she whispered.

Without hesitating, Owen captured her mouth once again, questing and stroking with his tongue as he reached between their bodies to undo the closures of his trousers. At the same time, she tried to turn and lift her hips to slide free of her own underthings, and they fumbled and tangled together until somehow he was on top of her, his cock hard and insistent between her legs.

He paused then, raising up on his elbows. "Are you ready for me? We can slow down."

"Oh, don't stop. Please."

He laughed, softly, and pushed inside her until his full length was achingly, exquisitely filling her. There was only this connection, only Owen's body and hers moving and straining together. He thrust deeply again and again until she was gasping for breath, her fingers gripping hard against his broad, strong shoulders. As if from far away, she heard Owen cry out, felt him tensing around her. The sound of his raw, rough pleasure sent her spinning, and she was adrift, at sea on a vast wave of sensation.

They washed back to the shore, their skins flushed and their breathing labored. Jo kissed his stubbled cheek. "Thank you," she said, smiling. "That was ... lovely."

He grinned back at her. "You're quite welcome, ma'am." He returned her kiss with a playful peck on her forehead. "And I promise not to be in such a hurry next time."

Next time. Jo's mind, which had been so peacefully wiped clear just a few seconds earlier, began to race. How many next times did he have in mind? Would he stay? For how long?

She forced herself to take a deep breath. Even after all of Owen's kisses, the bitter taste of the smoke she'd inhaled yesterday lingered in her mouth. Now was not the time for big decisions, not when she hadn't even changed out of last night's clothes. Things would seem much clearer after a bath, a fresh dress, and a good meal.

He cleared his throat. "I'm also sorry I haven't taken more care to ... ah, hell. I may as well be blunt. To avoid getting you pregnant."

"I don't think it's something we need to worry about. I never fell pregnant during my marriage, so it's likely that I'm simply not able to." She spoke as matter-of-factly as possible, but she kept her face firmly buried in his shoulder during this little speech. "Just another thing I can't fix."

"There's nothing about you that needs fixing," he said quietly. "I just want ... I want to make you happy. I want you exactly as you are." He pressed a kiss onto her forehead. "And I don't want to give you up. Come back to Vancouver with me."

She froze. "That's ... Owen, there's no reason to rush into anything. I've never even been to Vancouver."

"I mean it. This place doesn't exactly seem safe." Considering the very recent arson next door, Jo could hardly argue that point. "And I'll introduce you to everyone, show you the sights, take care of everything." The idea had clearly just occurred to him, and he sounded so excited.

She laughed a little nervously. "I couldn't even afford a hotel right now. There's the front window, and now the damage from the fire. And Doc will need so much help."

"Is that all?" He nuzzled her ear playfully. "You'd stay with me, obviously. I won't even charge you."

"That's ... You know I couldn't do that."

"What, stay with me? Why not? We're together right now. And it's not as if I have a bevy of domestic servants to gossip all over town."

"I just couldn't. Not without …"

"Without what?"

"Without being married. Or at least engaged."

That clearly wasn't what he had been expecting. "Ah. The thing is … That is, I'm definitely not marriage material. Not yet, I mean." He sounded genuinely regretful. "I think if I can write a good enough article about this place, and the arson, that'll put my career onto an entirely higher level. But who knows how long it'll be before I can make the kind of money I'd need to support a wife."

His excuses were beginning to ramble, so Jo silenced him with a quick kiss. "It's okay. I'm not asking you to marry me."

Still, it stung more than it should have that he had said "a wife," not her specifically. But that was irrational. It wasn't as if she actually wanted him to propose; she'd said herself that things were moving too quickly. And living with him in Vancouver was just a spontaneous thought that he'd blurted out. It was sweet of him, really.

"You don't need to worry about me or take care of anything. Let's just enjoy this morning."

And they did.

• • •

Owen's walk back to the St. Alice after breakfast should have been met by murmurs of disapproval. He was still wearing yesterday's singed, stained clothes, and there were very few respectable explanations for that. But the fire seemed to have put the citizens of Fraser Springs in charity with the world — the few people he passed smiled, and two even stopped him to shake his hand. The desk clerk at the hotel greeted him as if he were visiting royalty. He was in his room just long enough to strip down for a quick scrub at the washstand and to change into fresh clothes.

Back at Wilson's, the girls were already sweeping up outside and scrubbing soot off the bathhouse's siding. He sat down at a plank bench in the dining room still crowded with the breakfast rush. A cup of coffee seemed to magically materialize in front of him.

"How you feeling?" asked someone.

"There's the man of the hour!" called someone else. He waved back.

Usually, Owen loved the attention, but today it just felt like background noise. His mind was swarming with what felt like a million thoughts, most of them connected to Jo. Waking up this morning with her in his arms had felt so right. Better than right.

After Ilsa assured him that Jo would be kept in bed all morning — by force, if necessary — he returned to the hotel and redressed his arm, sent a telegram to his publisher, and set himself to drafting the outlines of his new article. He didn't labour over choosing the right phrases. He simply wrote. Page after page. Not a husky dog or a twelve-year-old protagonist in sight, but words that felt powerful and genuine. For the first time in years, he felt that he was writing something that mattered. An hour passed in this way, then two. Had he missed lunch? He definitely needed coffee — his eyes felt gritty, heavy...

He woke up with a start. The pencil was still in his hand, but he'd fallen asleep with his head on the desk, pillowed on the loose sheets of paper. Someone was knocking at the door.

"Mr. Wister! Are you okay, Mr. Wister?"

It took him a few seconds to remember who Mr. Wister was. His alter ego had died in the fire. How to explain *that* to the good people of Fraser Springs?

The hotel's bellboy was on the other side of the door; he looked relieved when Owen finally opened it.

"Telegram, sir," he said.

Owen tipped him and sat down on the bed.

Thank God for your safety STOP Will send cameraman to take article photos STOP Be there 24-48hrs

Owen smiled at the way his publisher unquestioningly jumped into action on his behalf. If Owen said he was writing an article that would set Vancouver on its ear, then D. W. Harrison — "Dubs" to his friends, and Owen was among those lucky few — took him at his word.

He tossed the telegram on the table, and his eye was drawn to the drifts of scribbled-on paper on its surface and on the floor around his feet. Well. It seemed his writer's block was well and truly broken. Dubs would be thrilled. Hell, *he* was thrilled; it was almost as exhilarating as surviving yesterday's fire. In fact, he'd felt more vital in the past few days than he could remember feeling in years.

It wasn't just the fire—it was Jo. Her searching touch, her kisses, the way she challenged him, and the way she listened to him. She was the reason he felt so goddamn *alive* lately. This morning, she had told him not to worry about her, but he couldn't help but wonder how she was holding up, what she was thinking. There was the shock of the fire yesterday, and her strangely subdued reaction to his offer this morning. *Should* he have proposed? She hadn't seemed to want him to, and she'd been so understanding about his desire to avoid rushing into marriage.

Regardless, the fire and its aftermath had given him a new sense of clarity: he would risk his own life to keep her safe, without hesitation. A man would be a fool not to try to make himself worthy of a woman who made him feel like that. He would write this article and make sure it was the best damn thing he'd ever produced. Dubs would arrive tomorrow, and together they'd get him published in the best papers in Canada. Everything would work out. He pulled a clean piece of paper from the sheaf, sharpened his pencil, and got back to work.

Chapter 23

Owen's publisher was younger than Jo expected. She'd imagined someone who looked like Doc Stryker, if he were an actual doctor. Instead, Owen arrived at Wilson's with a dapper little man in his mid-forties who radiated the nervous energy of a terrier. He wore a carnation in the buttonhole of his perfectly tailored suit and carried a cane topped with a silver eagle's head.

"Jo, this is my publisher and good friend, D. W. Harrison," Owen said. "I thought he was sending a cameraman, but it turns out—"

"Photography is a science and an art. Our many able cameramen understand the science, but the art ..." Harrison brushed some imaginary lint off his lapel. "Besides, I've known this man since he could barely grow facial hair, and I heard he'd gotten himself into yet another scrape."

"It's good to see you, too, Dubs," Owen said. "And Dubs, this is Jo."

Mr. Harrison gave a small smile and a quick touch to the brim of his perfectly brushed hat. "A pleasure. I've heard a great deal about you."

She could see instantly what a man like Mr. Harrison would think of a place like Fraser Springs, but Owen was all puppy-dog energy, rambling on about the layout of the town's buildings and introducing "Dubs" to Nils, Ilsa, and the other girls. Harrison proclaimed most of it "rustic" or "full of character," but only Ilsa seemed to impress him.

By the time the tour was finished, the dining room was packed for the lunch rush. Jo turned around to see that Harrison had pulled a chair into the middle of the room and climbed up on it.

"Can I have your attention, everyone? Everyone, can I have some silence?"

All the miners and her girls looked up at him, puzzled.

"Yes. Thank you. Now, my name is D. W. Harrison, and I have come to capture the true essence of this town in photographs of the highest quality. To do so, I will need your assistance. The way I see it, we have a classic hero's tale. The demented villain, the hero who rushes in to save the damsel in distress, and the townspeople who rise to the occasion in a time of great danger."

"Indeed!" Jo looked over to see that Mrs. McSheen had somehow appeared, as if the word "photographs" had conjured her. She sighed. This was going to get out of hand.

"The part of the heroine will be played by Miss Ilsa Pedersen."

"But I wasn't the one who—" Ilsa said.

"Yes, yes," Harrison interrupted. "But Mrs. Wilson is still recovering from the shock of her ordeal. And besides, people don't read newspapers for reality. They read them for excitement. For drama. We are capturing the *essence* of this event. If you think about it, that's more real than what actually happened. And Miss Pedersen beautifully captures the pristine spirit of Fraser Springs. Once our readers associate your town with such youth and beauty, you'll have to beat them away from the door with a stick." He made a striking motion with his cane.

There were several seconds of confused silence after this proclamation, followed by a low murmur of muttered discussion throughout the dining room.

"Now hold on a minute, Dubs!" Owen objected over the growing noise.

"No, it's a fine idea," Jo said loudly enough to silence the room. "I would prefer to stay out of the limelight."

She had to admit that it was impressive watching Harrison work. Fraser Springs was instantly being transformed before her eyes into a theatre set.

Harrison's cheeks were pink with enthusiasm. "Now, where is this Rusty character?"

"The RCMP took him to Nelson. They're transferring him to a jail in Vancouver," Mrs. McSheen said. "And may I say, Mr. Harrison, that I have extensive amateur theatrical experience and shall gladly volunteer my services if needed."

"Well, that's a stroke of luck on both fronts, ma'am. The warden is a good chum, and I'm sure he'll let me take some shots of Rusty. But just in case, do we have a volunteer who could play Rusty? Perhaps you there? With the beard? Could I trouble you to show me your teeth, sir? That's it. Make a snarl like a wolf."

Several miners showed their teeth, auditioning for their big break.

"If I may, Mr. Harrison?" Jo asked. "If one of these men plays Rusty, won't he face difficulties down the road if someone recognizes him from the newspaper and thinks he's actually an arsonist?"

Dubs sniffed. "I don't foresee that being a problem. We'll comb up his hair and put some shoe blacking on his face, and he will no longer look like himself at all. But your concern, dear lady, is noted. Now, we'll need to recreate the heroic rescue of Miss Pedersen."

"I'm not writing an article about myself," Owen said. "Come on, Dubs, that would be obscene. I don't want to appear in this at all."

"You're right. You're right. When I see a story, I sometimes go charging a little too eagerly after it. Like a hound on the scent of a rabbit. But that's better. Mystery man saves woman from burning building. Our hero is selfless. But when we let it slip that it's Vancouver's most eligible bachelor, Ow—"

"Ross Wister," Owen said hurriedly.

"Our man Ross Wister, well, let's just say that someone is about to get even more popular. Not that you weren't already, old chum." Owen was red-faced now, but he didn't object.

In just fifteen minutes, the fire that Jo could still see every time she closed her eyes had become a farce. Ilsa was playing her. Doc Stryker had been edited out. Doc's bar had turned into a sweet shop, since Dubs said that a woman like Ilsa would never be caught in a bar. (Jo couldn't manage to hold back a little laugh at that one). Even Mrs. McSheen had a role. She was going to be photographed standing next to the rubble of Doc Stryker's bar wearing her best sashes, a personification of the town's fundraising efforts.

If this version of the story brought publicity to Fraser Springs, they all would benefit. Still, she couldn't get out of her mind the way Mr. Harrison had looked at her when Owen had introduced them. Or rather, the way he had dismissed her. Owen was the hero, Ilsa was the younger, more beautiful version of herself, and Jo was simply a poor widow without even Mrs. McSheen's sashes to lend her distinction. If this was what people in Vancouver were like, she would gladly stay in the backwoods of Fraser Springs forever.

• • •

It was so good to see Dubs. They'd met shortly after Owen had moved to Vancouver. It was an unlikely friendship. Dubs was a decade older than Owen and moved in the city's wealthiest circles. Owen was fresh off the farm, without much more to recommend him to the world than a carpetbag full of notebooks. But the two men shared a love of the written word and a lively curiosity about the world. Owen wrote stories, while Dubs had a flair for making real life just as exciting as any novel.

After the impromptu meeting at Wilson's, the two men retreated to Owen's room at the St. Alice Hotel. Dubs materialized a flask from his waistcoat pocket and poured them each a brandy.

"To the man of the hour," Dubs said.

"Cheers," Owen said, clinking his glass with Dubs's.

Owen closed his eyes as he took a sip. After a week of Doc Stryker's hooch, the brandy felt like silk on his throat, which was still raw from smoke and cinders. When Owen re-opened his eyes, Dubs was staring at the seeping bandage on his arm.

"With any luck, that'll get you a handsome scar to show at parties," he said. "Before I left, I told Cynthia the vague outlines of the story, and she almost fainted. When you get back, she wants to throw you a party."

Owen made a face. Cynthia, Dubs's wife, was a lovely woman whose greatest joy in life seemed to be hosting elaborate, deathly formal dinner parties.

"I'm sure Cynthia would be delighted. Not so sure I'll be able to talk Jo into it, though."

Dubs stared out the window for a few moments. "Is that how things are between you and Mrs. Wilson, then?"

"I'll be straight with you. I've never felt so seriously about a woman in my life. Things are a bit up in the air at the moment, but I've asked her to come back to Vancouver with me."

"In which case, I congratulate you." He lifted his glass in Owen's direction. "She's a lovely woman, no two ways about that. Although ... I hesitate to mention this, Owen, I truly do. But do you think that'd be entirely *fair* to Mrs. Wilson?"

"What?"

Dubs took a sip of his brandy. "Transplanting a country mouse like that to Vancouver. I know you've had your fun here, but I can't imagine she's going to be very happy in the city."

"Jo's no mouse. She'd travel 'round the world and never turn a hair. And what's she got to be afraid of in Vancouver? Playing bridge with Cynthia? Trying to get caught up on five years of gossip in five days?"

Dubs took another sip. "You've hit the nail on the head, dear boy. Gossip. There are certain juicy tidbits that seem sure to follow her to town. Famed author Owen Sterling announces his engagement to a widowed masseuse who's been working her fingers into backwoods miners for years? Not to mention those rumours about the entire establishment being the worst sort of whorehouse. Do you think that Cynthia's really going to say, 'Splendid! I'll call on her at once!'?" Dubs's voice was level.

"That's unkind."

"I'm not trying to be unkind. I'm telling you this not just as your publisher but also as a friend. You have to admit that I've sanded some of your rough edges, and you've ... well, thanks to you, I can now go for a hike in the woods without getting eaten by mountain lions. So long as those woods are Stanley Park." He looked to Owen, expecting a laugh, and when he didn't get one, he took another sip and continued. "Marriage is a social contract. That's all I'm trying to say. A man's wife should help to raise his standing in society. Give him a bit of polish. You're a good-hearted man. Spontaneous. I've always liked that about you. But when it comes to marriage, a man needs to look very carefully before he goes a-leaping."

"And you need to get to know Jo before you start judging her."

"Which is another excellent point. How well do *you* know her? Who are her family? What do the finances look like in that establishment of hers?"

Owen opened his mouth to fire back, to defend both Jo and his own intelligence. Dubs was out of line, but damn it, he was also right. Owen didn't know if Jo had siblings or parents living. He didn't know much about her marriage to Albert Wilson. Didn't even know her maiden name. As to the bathhouse finances, he knew the place wasn't *thriving*, exactly, but beyond that?

His silence seemed to be answer enough for Dubs, who nodded. His publisher had always been good at knowing when to drop an argument at the precise moment he'd won it. "At any rate, it's good to see you ready to write again, my boy, even if you did try to get yourself half-cooked in the process. Let's go get your beauty shots, and then we can figure out where a man can buy something stronger than lemonade around here."

Chapter 24

By noon the next day, Jo had finally convinced Ilsa — who seemed to have declared herself a combination of nursemaid and jailer — that she could rest almost as effectively sitting at her desk as in her bed. And she would be in a *much* better mood at her desk, which seemed to decide the argument in her favor. How strange to think that just a few days ago, Owen had first kissed her in this room. She could practically feel his hands on her hair...

Just then, a sharp knock on the doorframe made her jump. She may have been daydreaming about Owen, but his *publisher* was the very last person in the world she wanted to see. Still, there he was, standing in the open doorway to her office with his perfectly trimmed little beard and a fresh flower in his lapel.

"I hope I haven't caught you at an inconvenient time, Mrs. Wilson?"

He had, rather. She was wearing one of her least flattering dresses and had ink stains all over hands. Nevertheless, she was glad he had found her in her office rather than the kitchen or the treatment rooms. Conducting business in the office allowed her to channel Albert: authoritative, businesslike yet warm, shrewd yet compassionate. In the short time they'd been married, Albert Wilson had taught her so much.

"Of course." She flashed her best "business smile": friendly but not too friendly. "I'm free for at least the next half-hour or so. Is this about the article, Mr. Harrison?" She rose to shake his hand across the desk.

He took the chair across from her, unbuttoning his fine suit coat as he sat. "Oh, not as such. My work's mostly done on that front."

"Then you were able to get the photographs you needed?"

"Yes indeed. And I'm sure they will turn out beautifully. Your Ilsa was a very capable artist's model."

"I look forward to reading the story in the paper. Will you be staying in Fraser Springs for much longer?" She could not keep a bit of chill from creeping into her tone.

Mr. Harrison's tone, too, was coldly polite. "Just another day or two, I think. But before I leave, I'd like to speak to you about something other than the story."

She tried to hide her surprise by straightening her posture a bit in the big leather chair. "Certainly. What would you like to know, Mr. Harrison?"

"I noticed that your front window is boarded up."

"Yes. There was an unfortunate accident."

He nodded and walked to the window to look out over Fraser Springs. "I imagine you'd like to get that fixed. I have to hand it to you: I've been in business for twenty-five years, and I've rarely seen an operation run as smoothly as yours."

Somehow, it didn't sound like a compliment. She merely gave a noncommittal, "Oh?"

Mr. Harrison turned back around, smiling broadly. "This ... affair with Owen." He made a vague gesture. "You've set yourself up beautifully."

"I'm afraid I don't follow." It took all of her professionalism to keep her tone even.

"The brick, the seduction, the fire. I couldn't have scripted it better myself, and I've been muckraking since before you were born."

Jo stood, her hands pressed flat on the desk in front of her. "Are you accusing me of something, Mr. Harrison?"

"Oh no, no, no. No accusations. Just observing, one professional to another. And you are *very* good, Mrs. Wilson. I'm sure we both see the same qualities in Owen. He's sentimental, he's impulsive, he wants so very much to help people and do the right thing. That's why I sent him up here. Saving some lost girls in the wilderness was the perfect way to jolt him out of this nasty round of writer's block, get his mind off reporting and back into the drama of the fiction game."

The man's roundabout meaning was becoming clear. "You knew all along that my bathhouse wasn't a brothel. You intentionally sent him here on a wild goose chase."

Mr. Harrison smiled. "Sometimes a small failure can deliver a healthy shock to the system. I intended no mischief towards *you*, Mrs. Wilson. I certainly never thought he'd get himself tangled up so seriously." He picked up the brick on her desk, testing its heft in his palm. Then he set it back down again. "It's so hard for a woman alone to make a living. You do what you have to do to survive. You reeled him in perfectly, but unfortunately, it's my duty to tell you that it ends here."

Seething anger replaced her confusion. "Are you implying that I'm some sort of ... confidence artist? That I've schemed my way into Owen's affections?"

"Oh, my dear. 'Scheme' is such an ugly little word. Indeed." His smile faltered; he seemed genuinely troubled by her choice of words. "I don't wish to imply anything *criminal*. Any woman in your position would make a grab for that particular brass ring. I'm merely cautioning you that if you think that this affair is going to end in marriage and a baby carriage, you're mistaken."

"But *Owen* was the one who asked me to ..." The words came out of her mouth before she had a chance to bite them back.

Mr. Harrison remained unruffled. "I'm not surprised that he may have... entangled himself a bit. You're a lovely woman, Mrs. Wilson. But I think I am safe in assuming that he did not offer you a proposal of marriage?"

Jo felt her jaw tighten. "I don't see how that is any of your concern." An awful thought occurred to her: exactly how much had Owen told his publisher about their affair? The idea of this stranger knowing her most intimate actions was horribly lowering. Owen wouldn't do that, would he? But why else would Mr. Harrison have come to see her?

He looked at her steadily. "Mrs. Wilson, you have been acquainted with Owen for a week. I've known him for fifteen years. I suppose, for example, that he hasn't yet told you about Anne McKinnet?" He waited for an answer, and so she gave a small, tight shake of her head. Another lover, perhaps? Oh, God ... a fiancée? Is *that* why he'd been so awkward and hesitant when she'd mentioned marriage that morning after the fire? "Such a pretty little thing, from one of the best families. Plays the harp, I believe. He courted her single-mindedly a couple of years back. But then, out of the blue, it became very important for him to spend three months alone in the woods writing his next book. Suddenly, he needed total peace and quiet, and he needed it so badly that he simply wrote her a letter and left town. It was quite a little scandal until her mama arranged an engagement to a nice young doctor."

"Owen was never so vulgar as to tell me about his history with other women."

"Of course, of course. But I ask you to consider, honestly, what happens if *you* find yourself abandoned, without family or your business here to fall back on?"

All the Wilsons on the walls in their gilded frames seemed to be smirking in assent with Mr. Harrison. Owen wouldn't leave out of meanness, but what seemed so right in a grotto sometimes didn't translate when the real world intruded. All she knew about Owen Sterling was that he was brave, and gentle, that he kissed her like she was necessary to his survival. And that he had come to town under false pretenses and was already ready to leave. She'd met the type before: men comfortable with running into a burning building, but not so good with the slow, painful rebuilding after the fire was put out.

"I don't say this to insult you," Mr. Harrison said. "But you have to know that Owen needs change. Novelty. Adventure. Always has. He wants to throw away a perfectly respectable career to become a muckraker, for God's sake. What do you think happens to you when his wanderlust sets in again? He'll rush away as quickly as he rushed in." His words were so close to thoughts that she herself had had about Owen, but coming from him they sounded cynical. Hurtful.

Jo took a deep breath. Outside, the lake was calm and the sky was cloudless. She suddenly felt just as calm. It was clear what she had to do.

"You're right. Owen is a grown man who makes his own decisions. I can give you my word that I won't pressure him to stay if he wants to leave."

Mr. Harrison nodded once and rose briskly to his feet. "Well then," he said. "I'm relieved to see that you're so reasonable on this subject. And this little chat has taken a great deal of worry from my mind when it comes to my friend's future. Thank you, Mrs. Wilson." He tipped his bowler and headed to the door.

The "little chat" with Mr. Harrison didn't change anything, really. He'd only told her what she'd already known about Owen. He was impulsive and not likely to make the kind of commitment she'd need from a man if she were to even begin to consider uprooting her life. Things were so unsettled in Fraser Springs that it seemed wisest to stay the course and take care of her business and her girls. She would simply have to be grateful for the time she had with him, without foolishly hoping for more. She rolled her neck to relieve the tension that had built up in the past quarter-hour, settled back into her chair, and got to work on the accounts.

Chapter 25

In the two days since the fire, Jo had barely managed to get more than a few words alone with Owen. He'd been constantly surrounded by his new admirers or holed up in his room with his publisher, writing that article for the papers. If she were being entirely honest with herself, she'd been a bit hurt that he hadn't made more of an attempt to see her. So when he walked into her office, she wasn't quite able to keep the foolish smile off her face as she stood to greet him.

"Owen, it's such a pleasure to—" Before she could finish the sentence, he crossed the few short steps to her desk, wrapped her in his arms, and captured her lips in a deep, searing kiss.

She pressed against him with a speed and ease that almost embarrassed her, slipping her hands around his shoulders and up to tangle in his thick, golden hair. He gave a little groan of pleasure as she nipped at his lower lip, and swept his own hands down the small of her back to pull her even more tightly against him.

"I came here to ask you something, but damn if I can remember it now," he murmured after they finally broke apart to catch their breath. She giggled into his neck. She, Josephine Wilson, *giggled*. Good Lord.

"Can I ask you something else?"

"Anything."

"Does that door lock?"

. . .

A little while later, as they set their rumpled clothing to rights, Jo found herself play-fighting Owen for the handful of hairpins he was holding hostage.

"But I like your hair down. I think I've earned some concessions, don't you?"

"Stop it!" She tried to sound stern and businesslike, but she kept slipping up and laughing. "I can't go downstairs like this."

"Then don't go downstairs. We'll have our meals delivered to your room for the rest of the week, and you can issue your orders from the bathtub. Like Marie Antoinette."

With a final lunge, she captured the hairpins. "Ha!" Owen held his hands up in mock surrender.

She turned away to the window looking out over the lake, attempting to use the glass as a makeshift mirror. She pinned her hair into a decent semblance of a chignon and turned back to see a suddenly solemn Owen staring back at her.

"I have to leave soon, you know. I've been putting it off as long as I can, but I need to be in Vancouver when the article runs. And I've got a dozen invitations and commitments I've been dodging too long already."

"Oh." This wasn't a surprise, of course, but her throat tightened anyway. "When is 'soon,' exactly?"

"Tomorrow? The day after that, at the absolute latest."

He came up behind her and wrapped her in his arms, resting his chin on the crown of her head.

"Tell me you've thought about my offer."

"I have. I still don't want to live in Vancouver."

"Then to hell with Vancouver. We could go anywhere together. New York. Paris. Shanghai, if that strikes your fancy."

"Be serious, Owen. I meant that I don't want to live anywhere else at all."

"I am serious. You'll never get a better chance to sell this place than after my article comes out. I sing its praises quite a bit, so you're sure to find a buyer."

She pulled free of his arms, needing to look him in the face. "You're not listening. I don't want to leave right now, and I definitely do not want to sell my home right now. I finally have a chance to see what this business can be without the moral crusaders breathing down my neck every day."

"Honey, you can't honestly want to work yourself to death in a backwater like this for the rest of your life."

The condescension in his voice raised her hackles immediately. "I take *pride* in my work!"

"Pride doesn't mean a thing if you can't sleep at night. I don't come from money, darling. My father was a chicken farmer. He spent his entire life grubbing away at it, too proud to walk away from a doomed enterprise. It may be honest, but it kills you by inches. Every year, *that* was going to be the year he finally broke even. He died when I was nineteen. The only time that damned place turned a profit was when I sold it, right after the funeral.

"I think you're scared," he continued. "You got married because it was the safe thing to do. You stayed on here because it was safe. Maybe you even surrounded yourself with other women because it made you feel safe."

"And you're so brave, is that it? You're going to rescue me from my life?"

"You're meant for brave things, Jo!"

"You think it doesn't take courage to run this place?"

"Jo, listen to what I'm telling you. It's not pride; it's cowardice. You have to stop being a martyr for your dead husband's dying business."

There was a breathless little pause as she absorbed the blow. He had no right, no right at all, to speak of the most difficult decisions of her life in such a crass way.

"I'm not going to stand here and let you insult me like that." She tore herself free of the circle of his arms, turned away from his gaze, and headed for the door.

"Jo," he said softly. "Jo, stop for a minute." And God help her, she stopped, exactly where she stood. She was so angry, and a foolish part of her still wanted him to take her in his arms, to re-establish that easy sweetness they'd had between them just a little while ago.

"I'm sorry. I don't mean to insult you." But he didn't move, didn't reach for her.

She breathed out slowly. "Can we compromise on this somehow? You could leave and take care of the article and then come back. Or we could write."

"I don't want to be pen pals, Jo. And it doesn't sit right, leaving you here without me."

"Why not? It's not as if I'll get engaged to another man while you're away," she shot back.

His brows snapped together. "What?"

She shook her head, as if that could clear the specter of perfect, jilted Anne McKinnet from her mind. "It doesn't matter. I just don't understand why this has to be everything or nothing, right this minute."

He crossed his arms. "How long did you wait before you married Wilson?" It was precisely the wrong thing to say. Albert's proposal had been sudden, yes, and she'd accepted him immediately. But her decision had been made in a moment of fear and vulnerability, and it was only by pure luck that her marriage had been as loving as it had been.

"That's different."

"Because he owned a successful business."

"That's not why. I *needed* to marry Albert."

"And you don't *need* to be with me?"

"You're twisting my words."

"Then I'll be as plain as I can, Jo. Do you want to be with me, yes or no?"

"I ... I don't *know*, Owen. It's too soon."

"Just answer the question."

"It's not a matter of *wanting* you. I have responsibilities. I can't just abandon them on a whim."

"I'll take care of you."

"So I'll be your responsibility, the kind you'd never abandon on a whim?"

"Yes. I mean, no. God *damn* it, now who's twisting words?"

"Maybe I *will* sell this place one day. But it won't be because a man snaps his fingers and tells me to trot along behind him. " She was shouting now. Dear God, how was it possible that this was going so badly wrong so quickly? Falling in love was supposed to be effortless, but when it came all tangled up with fear and uncertainty, it became the most difficult thing in the world. Anger, however, was simple.

"You can't have it both ways, Owen! You can't ask me to abandon my life right this minute and then ask me to wait until *you're* ready to start a new one. I've *fought* for my place in this town. You helped me fight for it. I didn't run away then, and I'm not running away now. Or ever."

They glared at each other until he gave up and scrubbed his hands over his face.

"So that's what I was for you? A way to help save your business? Or maybe just a nice little roll in the hay before you got back to work."

She hadn't thought Owen — cheerful, sunny Owen — capable of the sneer currently twisting his face. Her right palm itched with the urge to slap him. But she'd never laid angry hands on anyone in her life, and she wasn't about to start now.

"I think you should leave. Now."

"Good. I've clearly overstayed my welcome." He snatched his coat from the back of the armchair. "I won't bother you. Ever again."

She didn't answer. Instead, she turned to look out the window, her arms hugged tightly to her chest, tucking herself completely inward and away from him. Her body was curled like a question mark, but there were no questions anymore. They'd both made themselves abundantly clear.

He slammed the front door loudly on his way out.

Chapter 26

Owen stood in the lobby of the St. Alice, awkwardly accepting compliments and returning tips of the hat. He couldn't wait for Dubs to meet him for breakfast. After the night he'd had, he needed to talk to someone with a steady head on his shoulders. Dubs had never steered him wrong before. It also wasn't like Dubs to be late.

Twenty minutes later, Dubs bustled in.

"I was starting to give you up for dead," said Owen. "Is everything all right?"

Dubs gave him a long-suffering look. "It's been an interesting morning."

The details came out over the St. Alice's dry-as-sand scones, which both men picked at.

"This gives me no pleasure, my boy. I wanted to follow your advice and get to know Jo a bit. I've seen too many good men brought down by ... unsuitable women. So I went to see her this morning." Owen leaned forward in his chair. That dismissive crack Jo had made about getting engaged to another man while he was gone suddenly made more sense.

"You told her about Anne, didn't you?"

Dubs raised his hands defensively. "I thought you might have already told her. She didn't carry on about it. Took it quite well, actually."

"What did you tell her, *exactly*," Owen pressed.

"I may have been overly direct, to be honest. I put it quite bluntly: that you had courted Anne and left her in the lurch when it came time to propose."

It was a *very* blunt statement of what had happened. "I didn't 'leave her in the lurch'! I had a book to finish. How was I supposed to support a wife otherwise? I didn't know it was going to turn into such a ... a ..."

"Call it what it was: a scandal. Anne was damned lucky to land that Smythe boy afterwards." Owen slumped back in his chair, like a sullen boy being lectured by an older brother.

"Damn it. The next time you get an urge to help me with women? Don't."

"Oh, don't sulk. That business with Anne is the least of your worries when it comes to Mrs. Wilson." He stared fixedly into his coffee cup.

"Dubs! Out with it!"

"Frankly, she doesn't seem all that broken up that you're leaving. She's a widow, and she was lonely. These things happen all the time. She made it quite clear to me that her business is a lot more important to her than whatever mutual arrangement the two of you may have had."

She'd made it quite clear to him as well. She'd been so angry with him, so dismissive. "That's flattering. Anything else?"

"I told her that you wouldn't be happy in Fraser Springs, and that she wouldn't be happy in Vancouver."

"And ... did she agree with that?"

"Yes. She did." Owen must have looked as gutted as he felt, because Dubs reached across the table to grip his forearm. "I'm sorry to be the bearer of bad news. I didn't realize you were so serious about the gal."

It was time to take the hint. Jo had told him, and now his oldest friend had told him the same thing.

Dubs coughed into the silence stretching between them. "At any rate, if we leave now, we can still catch the slow boat out of here today. We'll be back in civilization before you know it."

Owen drained the last, cold dregs from his coffee cup with a grimace. "Good. I'll start packing."

• • •

The process of returning to Vancouver was easier than Owen anticipated. Within twenty minutes, the hotel bill had been paid and he was up in his room packing. It was so easy to fold Ross Wister's life away.

Two heavy wool suits. Five pairs of drawers. Five undershirts. One sweater. One shaving kit. Two pairs of trousers. Three button-down shirts. Five collars and ten cuffs. One dime-store novel. One botanical history guide whose pages he had never even cut, let alone read. These were the things Ross Wister had taken with him to Fraser Springs, and these were the things Owen Sterling was now packing. They smelled of sweat and smoke. They smelled of mint salve.

They smelled of her.

And now they were neatly folded in a trunk going back to Vancouver, where his laundry man would press the odours out of them until all they smelled of was starch. He looked around the hotel room. The novel Nils had loaned him was still on the bedside table, so he placed it on top of the rest of his gear, along with a smooth white pebble he'd pocketed in the grotto. Sentimental foolishness. He tossed the pebble into the wastepaper basket.

Owen shaved, focusing on the shush of the razor against his skin, and applied the aftershave, focusing on the salve's burn, and wrapped his arm in a clean bandage, focusing on wrapping the gauze evenly and tying a secure knot. And then he waited with Dubs in the lobby of the St. Alice Hotel, saying nothing, trying his best to nod politely and make small talk when townspeople offered their good wishes. Word of his leaving had traveled quickly through the town.

The porter brought coffee for them as they waited for the ship. He drank the thin, bitter brew and tried to cheer himself with the thought of how good the fare in Vancouver would taste compared to this. When he got back home, he would enjoy a slice of pie and a proper coffee at The White Lunch and maybe treat himself to a good supper at the Hotel Vancouver. A shave with hot towels at his favourite barber's shop, and then he'd pop by some of the clubs for a little sorely missed conversation. Yes, it would be good to get back to a real city.

He repeated that phrase—*it would be good to get back to a real city*—to himself over and over until he started to believe it. Enough of the mosquitos and the hot spring's sulfur odour. It would be good to hear trolleys and bicycle bells and car horns again. His bags checked with the clerk, he wandered slowly up the boardwalk, away from Wilson's, until he ran out of boards to walk. Somewhere along the way, Dubs had disappeared. He always knew when to give a fellow some space.

Owen tried hard to focus on the journey ahead of him, rather than searching the crowd for Jo. Instead, he noticed a figure slowly making his way down the boardwalk, using an old umbrella for a cane.

"Come to say goodbye, Doc?" Owen asked. Although his complexion remained pale and his gait was unsteady, Doc's fighting spirit was clearly back in force.

"Nah. Just came to see you in that plaid monkey suit one more time." The hand he rested on Owen's forearm was trembling, whether from emotion or fatigue Owen couldn't guess. "And to say thank you. Was too busy trying to catch my breath to properly thank you at the time."

"Don't mention it," Owen said. "I only did what anyone would do. You're looking better."

Doc smiled. "Got to be. I got to dance at your wedding, don't I?"

The words slugged Owen in the gut. "Oh. There's not ... That is, Jo made it clear I'm not ..."

Doc squeezed his hand. "Turned you down, did she? Can't say as I'm surprised, to be honest. Oh, well. She's stubborn as a mule, so you've got to be even more stubborn."

"She knows what she wants, and it's not me."

"What she wants! Ha!" The intensity with which he interrupted Owen sent Doc into a coughing fit. "She's not doing what she *wants*. She's doing what she believes is *right*. Give her some time." He coughed again and gripped Owen's arm, then looked straight into his eyes. "Don't give up on her out of pride is all I'm asking. Can you do that?"

Owen patted the hand that gripped his forearm. "Sure, Doc." No harm in letting a kind old man have some hope.

The SS *Minto*'s whistle gave several sharp screeches. "Sounds like my ride's about to leave," Owen said. "Goodbye. And good luck with the rebuilding."

Doc grinned. His eyes were watery from his coughing fit. "See you soon," he said.

• • •

Tomorrow, Jo would have to face all the polite conversations. "A pity Mr. Wister had to leave!" "We'll certainly miss Mr. Wister around these parts!" "Jo, how are you keeping?" Today, however, all she wanted was to be alone with her thoughts. And so she headed for the grotto.

But just when she needed it most, even the cool stone was no comfort. She had brought along her bathing costume, and the heavy mohair felt oppressive after years of bathing in her underthings. She leaned back against the rock and tried to clear her mind. It was no use. When she closed her eyes, she saw only Owen. The memory of their time in the grotto brought waves of regret, not pleasure. She opened her eyes.

"You are being ridiculous," she told herself aloud. "Stop mooning." The grotto turned her voice into an echo, until it seemed that a whole chorus of people were chiding her. The twisted spires of rock looked menacing today, like she was in the mouth of some creature about to clamp down on her. The blue waters and the pale stone only reminded her of a frigid wasteland. Even the cave paintings were just another reminder of how people made their brief impressions and then disappeared.

Owen would return to Vancouver. She would stay in Fraser Springs, maintaining Wilson's, chasing the tourism money, hoping that the mine didn't peter out too soon the way the one in Granite City had, and the one in Blakeburn before that.

The charred wreckage of Doc Stryker's would be turned into wood ash for fertilizer, and soon a new bar would be erected. And one day, inevitably, she would be reading the society pages and see the announcement: noted author Owen Sterling engaged to wed a fresh-faced little debutante. Someone suited to society living, who could be a hostess for literary salons and help Owen's career. Someone young and sparkling, who'd been following a bright, clear path from the schoolroom to the altar. No haunted dreams, no business to run, just an endless round of teas and afternoon callers and new frocks. She would have soft hands and sing like an angel. And she would have saved her virtue for her wedding night.

Jo's entire life took place in less than one square mile. She had not realized how small her life must look to someone like Owen. Or how small it now looked to her without someone to share it with.

She closed her eyes again, trying to distract herself by making a mental list of everything she would need to repair the bathhouse. The glass was the main concern, but maybe in the summer they could take the window out altogether and make the parlour an extension of the porch. No, that was silly. Maybe she could turn it somehow into two smaller windows. She sighed. Try as she might, the numbers never seemed to add up. Not in the account books and not in her life.

The smooth limestone pressed against the knobs of Jo's spine, reminding her of how Owen had once wrapped his arms around her, fanning his fingers against the small of her back to cushion her from the hard stone. If she closed her eyes, she could almost feel the pressure of his thighs against hers. The water was still now, but she could picture how the rhythm of their bodies had churned the water so it'd lapped against them. As they'd rested together afterwards, she had laid her head against his chest so that she could hear his heartbeat under the staticky fizz of the mineralized water. She saw him flushed and shining, smiling at her.

Stupid. She had been so stupid. But it had been a lovely holiday from her life. And all holidays end. As Jo rose out of the water, she heard a low hooting noise so faint she thought it might be a bird's cry. But, no, she would know that sound anywhere: the SS *Minto* had arrived. She dressed deliberately. She would *not* hide in the grotto until the boat was safely away. And she would also *not* give in to the urge to hurry, to run to the docks, to find Owen and beg him to forget everything she'd said. To beg him to stay. She had made the responsible decision, and she would abide by it. She was entirely calm. And yet her fingers were shaking as they fastened each fiddly button, each hook and eye, each tie. There was no mirror to judge whether she was presentable, so she ran her hands along her body to make sure at least the outer dress was secure. It was.

Jo walked out of the grotto, up the embankment, her heart thrumming in her throat. Little wet tendrils of hair clung to the back of her neck. Owen had stroked his fingers just there, so gently. She could picture in crystalline detail the constellation of little scars across his tanned arms and hands that told the tale of scrapes and misadventures. The strong chest that tapered into a narrow waist and hips. The way he looked at her.

No. Enough. She reached the edge of the bluff just in time to hear three sharp hoots. The steamboat pulled away from the dock.

No sign of Owen on the decks facing the shore or on the dock. He must truly be gone now. Her throat tightened. The only thing that kept her from weeping was the knowledge that her foolishness would not become gossip fodder for the town. She had not humiliated herself by racing down to the dock with petticoats dragging and hair askew, and she would not show a tearstained face to the world either.

From her vantage point on the bluff, she could see the whole town. One big hotel. A few small bathhouses. A general store. A bank. Rows of houses and tiny cabins peering like busybodies down at the boardwalk. The black scorch where Doc Stryker's had been. Not one of the townspeople scuttling about below looked up to where she stood. Even the girls at Wilson's went on without her: buying groceries, running errands, perfectly capable of coping. Not needed, Jo Wilson sat on top of the hill for a very long time as the town of Fraser Springs went about its business. She stayed until the SS *Minto* grew small on the horizon and then vanished from view. She stayed until the wind smoothed over the wake the boat left behind, until it seemed that the town was perfectly isolated, like a village in a Christmas snow globe.

Finally, she stood up and smoothed the front of her dress. She would set Owen Sterling out of her mind. She had friends who cared for her. She had her business, with employees and clients who depended on her and respected her. And she had her pride and her independence. That was all so much more than most people had. It was important to stay firm in the decisions you make in life, she decided. She just had to keep her eyes facing forward and her shoulders straight. She strode down the hill and back to Wilson's.

Part 2

Chapter 27

July 20, 1910

Dear Mrs. Wilson,

Over the past year, your fellow Fraser Springians (Springites? Springers?) sent you thirty-three of the nastiest letters I've ever laid eyes upon. Happily, those lies had the unintended consequence of bringing me to Fraser Springs and introducing me to you. But even though these slanderous letters played a role in our meeting, I cannot allow them to have the final word.

So I am sending you one more letter along with a small gift. I trust it arrived in one piece. I sold my article on Fraser Springs. Mr. Harrison was able to negotiate a handsome sum for it, and when I recalled your difficulty getting replacement glass for your broken window, it seemed to me that you should benefit from my good fortune. It is, after all, your story, and I hope that when you read my article, you will find that I did it justice.

Yours,

Owen Sterling

P.S. I am sadly short on bricks, so I hope you will accept conventional mail. If you would care to correspond, you can reach me care of the rooming house where I am staying, which I've listed below.

• • •

The Vancouver World - Front Page - Sunday Edition, August 9, 1910.

Identity of Hero Journalist Revealed

Last week, we published a Letter to the Editor from Mrs. Robert McSheen of Fraser Springs, which called on the publication to reveal Ross Wister's true identity so that he might be commended for his valiant actions.

In the end, we consulted with the man himself, and he gave us permission to reveal his real name. The truth of Ross Wister's identity may be shocking for those of you with young lads in the house, or those who enjoy reading adventure stories yourself, for Ross Wister is none other than famed novelist Owen Sterling.

Sterling is the author of over thirty adventure novels for boys, including *Trouble on the Mountain* and *Escape From Raven's Peak*. His stories are beloved by readers of all ages and have played a crucial role in inspiring our boys to engage in healthful outdoorsmanship. We here at *The Vancouver World* are proud to call Owen Sterling one of our own, and we intend to show this pride with a ceremony attended by our dear Mayor (and owner of *The Vancouver World*), The Honorable L. D. Taylor, to be held on Hastings Street on August 19 at one in the afternoon. All members of the public are welcome to attend.

The Vancouver World - Social Pages – September 1, 1910

Vancouver's Most Eligible Bachelors and How to Meet Them
By Miss Imogen Thornbush

Ladies, should you think that courting season is over just because we're putting away our picnic baskets and summer pastels, think again. Fall and winter have their own charms, and whose thoughts don't turn to romance when the seasons bring us harvest dances and cosy fireside chats?

The fact is plain: there is no wrong time to meet Mister Right. That is why I have taken the liberty of speaking to Vancouver's best and brightest in order to compile the most up-to-the-date list of our fair city's most eligible bachelors. Of course, we must not go hunting for men as if they were grouse in the woods. No, the art of courtship is one of refinement and subtlety. Sometimes, however, love needs a little push. If we sit at home working on our petit point today, we may soon find ourselves spending another summer chaperoning the 'dates' of our friends. Victory favours the bold, ladies!

So in this spirit, here is my list of Vancouverites to set your sights upon (and where to find them!).

First, and perhaps unnecessarily, we must draw your attention to celebrated author and real-life hero Owen Sterling. Mr. Sterling set our hearts aflutter when he rescued two people from a burning building (and was too modest to boast of his heroics!). When girls see his sparkling blue eyes and woodsman's physique, they practically pull each other's hair to get a seat at the table with him. Truly, he is the complete package. A man whose career is devoted to the thinking up of wholesome adventures is bound to be a devoted father, and you will never run out of conversation with this brainy fellow.

Though some might find his zeal for the muddy outdoors distasteful, he also moves in the finest circles. My sources tell me that in the past few weeks he's been spotted at a whirl of society dinners, galas, and fundraisers. Pluckier gals might also try to join him on Wednesday nights at the British Columbian Naturalist Society meetings. Hope you can tell your spotted owl from your black-tipped chickadee, girls!

Whatever you do, my advice is to ACT FAST if you want to become Mrs. Owen Sterling. A man like this won't remain single for long.

Chapter 28

Nine weeks without him, and yet Owen Sterling's voice had never left her head. It came through as she prepared salve or scrubbed floors or sought out knots in the pale, doughy backs of the rich women who came to see her now, their rosewater-scented bodies so different from those of the miners she was accustomed to. His voice came in the memories that even the smallest details of the bathhouse could trigger. The axe leaning against the wall was a reminder of the contest he'd had with Nils. The chipped enamel cup recalled all those times he'd sat in her dining room, inhaling the smell of coffee with his eyes closed. Sometimes a man with his physique would be sitting at the long slab table, and she'd forget he'd ever left. *Oh, there you are*, she found herself thinking. *So good to see you again.*

But, no, Owen was back in Vancouver. Sometimes she would dream that she was traveling on a tram down city streets past an endless scroll of buildings with advertisements painted on the sides, and dogs and horse carts and people running across the streetcar's path and alongside it, drifting in and out of her vision, not looking at her. No, she could never live in Vancouver.

Fraser Springs wasn't a bad place, really, nor was it hopelessly set in its ways. The same people who had penned acid-tongued hate letters now seemed genuinely happy to see her. They invited her to church group meetings, where she tried her best to swallow the dry cookies and the too-sweet lemonade, grainy with sugar crystals, and agree with Mrs. McSheen that, yes, business was booming, and yes, it was the Lord's work, and yes, also probably a little bit of Mrs. McSheen's work as well.

Jo was waking up earlier and earlier these days. She was dressed and downstairs well before dawn this morning. She was almost disappointed to see that, despite last night's larger-than-usual dinner crowd, the kitchen had been left spotless. Every surface gleamed in the flickering yellow gaslight. She sighed. Deep down, she knew that she could scrub the floor until it shone and the wood polish chapped her hands, but every time she looked up she would still imagine Owen walking in with Nils. She could rub coat after coat of wax on the long table, but it wouldn't stop her from picturing him sitting on the bench with the top button of his collar undone and his hair askew, joking over bacon and coffee.

It didn't matter. She tied on her apron, cinching the strings unnecessarily tight, and picked up the tin buckets they used to fill the big kitchen washtub. Hauling water in from the pump house was usually a chore they left for Nils or one of the other men, but this morning she very much needed the mental clarity that came from lifting heavy things.

By the time she made it back across the yard, with only half of the water sloshed onto her skirts, her breathing was heavier, but her racing thoughts had slowed. She stirred up the stove, hauled in a half-dozen loads of split firewood, and scrubbed enough potatoes to feed a small army. She'd begun cutting in lard for biscuits when Ilsa, muzzy and half-awake, silently joined her at the scarred countertop.

They worked together in silence for a while, Ilsa chopping the still-wet potatoes into chunks while Jo kneaded her mountain of dough.

Finally, Ilsa cleared her throat. "If that's biscuits, they'll be hard as rocks the way you're working them."

Startled, Jo looked down and experimentally pushed at the smooth white mass with the heel of her hand. It sprang back like

India rubber. Ilsa was right; it would be impossible to roll this out. She huffed in frustration, sending little eddies of flour swirling onto the floor. Abandoning the traitorous biscuits, she stalked across to the stove, jabbed at the coals, and slammed the largest of the cast iron lids into place. She winced at the loud clang that burst across the domestic tranquility of the kitchen.

"Jo. Stop," Ilsa said quietly. Jo took a deep, steadying breath before she turned around. "You've been running yourself ragged like this for weeks and weeks. Eventually you're going to have to tell me what went wrong."

"I am *aware* of that, Ilsa," she snapped.

There was another long silence, but she knew Ilsa well enough to recognize this one as punitive. She squeezed her eyes shut and forced herself to turn away from the red glow of the stove.

"I'm sorry. I shouldn't snarl at you just because I ... haven't been sleeping well." She could see the question on Ilsa's face as clear as if the pretty blonde had spoken it aloud. "For the thousandth time, I don't want to talk about Owen Sterling. I misjudged the situation, and that's all there is to it."

Ilsa left her potatoes to move the two biggest skillets onto the range to heat. Standing elbow to elbow with Jo, she asked, gently, "Did he hurt you?"

"I ... beg pardon?"

"Did he force himself on you?" Ilsa's voice was low. "Physically."

"What? No! No, of course not."

"Thank God for that, then. I didn't think he was that kind, but you never know." Ilsa's expression of relief was so plain and so sincere. Certainly she'd dealt with worse things than a man leaving her.

At a loss for words, Jo ran her fingers down the condensation on the edge of the washtub and flicked the moisture into the glossy black skillets, where the droplets instantly danced and sizzled away. There was still no motion from upstairs. The rest of the establishment seemed to have collectively decided that today was a holiday.

Together, the two women sliced bacon, boiled coffee, cut the god-awful biscuit dough into rounds and loaded them into the oven. Jo realized she had momentarily run out of useful tasks. More to keep her hands busy than anything, she ladled out two cups of strong, bitter coffee and handed one to Ilsa.

After a few silent sips, Ilsa asked, cautiously, "What did you misjudge, exactly? Why are you down here frying potatoes with me when you could be having breakfast in bed in Vancouver?"

Jo turned her blue-and-black enameled mug nervously in her hands. "Who did you hear that from?"

"Doc Stryker. He tried his best to keep his mouth shut, but I'm *very* charming."

Ilsa was the best friend she had, and she was right. Jo sighed. She had been shutting everyone out, trying to keep her disaster of an affair with Owen Sterling to herself. But Ilsa wouldn't judge her, surely. "We were ... intimate. More than once. And it was lovely. He was lovely. But he wanted more than I could give him."

"Well, some men do have strange tastes. I once knew a girl who had a regular caller who ..."

Jo did *not* want to hear the rest of this little anecdote. "He wanted me to go away with him to Vancouver. But he never said anything about marriage. Or ... or love."

Ilsa's expression was almost maternal. "Is that all? Lord, you had me thinking it was something against nature. Of course he fell in love with you. Any fool could tell that."

"But it isn't that simple! I have a *life* here. People depend on me, and I can't give all that up to go trailing after some man I barely know. Especially one who hasn't proposed and who's already lied to me once about who he is."

Ilsa took another slow sip. "Is that what you argued about so badly that he ran off back to the city? Giving up the business?"

"That's the only real option, isn't it? His whole life is in Vancouver."

"He could be a writer from anywhere, though, couldn't he?"

"I ..." Somehow, this thought had not occurred to her. It certainly wasn't traditional for a husband to move for a wife and not the other way around, but that didn't mean it was impossible. She shook her head sharply to jostle away the words "husband" and "wife."

"It was him that sent the new window, wasn't it?" Ilsa asked carefully. Jo shrugged.

"Jo! That must have cost him a fortune! Most of us only get some draggle-tailed carnations after we fall out with a beau."

"I know. It was a very thoughtful gift. But I haven't heard a single word from him since. He probably already fell in love with some pretty rich girl who read about him in that awful 'Eligible Bachelors' column. I don't need to be rejected a third time by the same man. I've washed my hands of him."

Another silence stretched out, but the air between them was so much more peaceful than before. After a few minutes of listening to the soft noises of boiling water and the first morning birds, Ilsa set her empty coffee cup down. It made a bright *plink* noise against the table. "Well, you know your own mind, and I'll never convince you to feel something you don't." She rose and walked around the table to Jo's chair, and placed her hands on Jo's upper arms. "Thank you for telling me what happened. Finally." She pulled Jo into a hug that had more forgiveness in it than most church sermons.

Jo returned the squeeze, smiling. Then she stood and took their cups back to the sink.

"Did you ever write him? To let him know you got the window?" Ilsa asked from the other side of the kitchen.

Jo sighed. Of course Ilsa had a parting shot. "I signed for the delivery."

"That's not the same thing, though, is it? He sent you a grand apology, and for all he knows, you smashed it into little bits." She shrugged dramatically. "Anyway. I'm going to go wake up Mary and the rest of the lazy cows. Your terrible biscuits are probably done by now."

Ilsa disappeared up the stairs. Jo dropped the cups into the sink and then stared out of the window without truly seeing anything.

Damn. It seemed she had a letter to write.

Chapter 29

There was nothing natural about the clubhouse of the Ontario Naturalist Society. The only wood in the room was holding up the bar, and that had been carved and lacquered and buffed until the grain was gone from it. The green velvet curtains made him feel claustrophobic, and the swags in the wallpaper reminded him of leering eyes.

"Owen?"

He hadn't been paying attention to what Dubs was saying.

"Sorry, Dubs. What was that?" Dubs was smoking a thin cigarillo, adding to the haze of smoke that seemed to hover over everyone in the room.

Dubs laughed at him good-naturedly. "Distracted by all the pretty girls who just happen to be so very interested tonight in the migratory pattern of wolves?"

Owen sighed. He glanced down at his notes for tonight's talk. He was halfway through his speaking tour, but the idea that all of these people wanted to hear him was still jarring. Tonight he would give a speech to the members of this small club, but tomorrow he would address the entire Canadian Parliament. The Naturalist Society had asked him to contribute to their effort to get the government to reconsider a bill to increase the wolf cull, which would devastate the wolf population. Apparently his moderate celebrity made him a more appealing spokesman than the tweedy old professors who formed the bulk of the Society's membership.

Usually these meetings attracted a small audience of those professor types, leavened by a smattering of laymen looking for a captive audience for tales of the insect collecting they did when stationed overseas during the Boer War. Today, however, young women made up the majority of the attendees, and they were all dressed for a gala, not a dry lecture.

"Looks like Ottawa has just as many science-minded young ladies as Vancouver and Toronto did," Dubs noted wryly. He had accompanied Owen on his tour, and Owen was grateful to have a friend in the audience.

"Wonderful." It seemed that blasted matrimonial column had preceded his arrival in every stop of this tour.

"Enjoy it while it lasts, Mr. Vancouver's Most Eligible Bachelor. Most men would give their right arm to have so many attractive women feigning interest in wolves just to speak to them."

Owen said nothing. Their conversation was interrupted by a pair of blond women wearing evening gowns that clung to their curves and dripped with lace.

"Good evening, ladies," said Dubs.

Owen managed a nod in their direction.

"Hello Mr. Sterling," the two girls said in unison.

"And who might you be?" asked Dubs.

"I'm Rebecca, and this is Eleanor," one of the girls said. Before Owen had a chance to say a word, Dubs had jumped to his feet to pull out the remaining two chairs at the table. The girls took the seats eagerly, utterly oblivious to the scowl Owen directed at his smiling publisher.

"We just wanted to ask you if your talk is going to be too scary," Eleanor said. She affected the breathless whisper of a much younger girl.

"Too scary?" Owen asked.

"I'm terribly afraid of wolves. I just don't know what I'd do if I ever saw one."

Eleanor and Rebecca fluttered their eyelashes, simpered, and generally flirted shamelessly. He knew it should be alluring, but their patter reminded him of Mrs. McSheen. He tried to imagine what Doc would say to these girls. Nils would probably just get up and walk away.

"Wolves are actually quite social creatures," Owen said. "I don't find them frightening in the least."

Eleanor—or was it Rebecca?—leaned closer to him, displaying an expanse of creamy bosom in the process. "Well that's because you're a *hero*. Why, I bet a wolf would regret it if he tried to tangle with you."

"I'm sure Owen would protect you from these fearsome creatures," said Dubs. "Wouldn't you?"

"Wolves won't harm you. In fact, they're exceedingly cautious animals. And they have a very interesting kinship structure."

One of the girls clapped her hands. "Do you mean they have little wolf families? Like a mommy and a daddy and a baby wolf?"

"Not ... exactly," Owen said. He glanced at Dubs in exasperation, but the man merely nodded at him encouragingly. No help to be had there. "Well, it was lovely to meet you ladies, but I need to review my speech. Will you excuse us?"

The girls huffed off. He was being rude, but his desire for small talk had dwindled into non-existence lately.

"Was it necessary to be so brusque?" Dubs asked after the girls were out of earshot.

"Yes," Owen said. "Is it necessary for you to keep encouraging them?"

"Just trying to help you out. The future Mrs. Sterling is going to pass right by while you stare at those scribbles."

"I wish to God people would stop mentioning 'the future Mrs. Sterling' to me," he grumbled.

"Well, pardon me for taking a friendly interest in your well-being."

"Oh, don't take it like that. I'm sorry for being such a bear. I'm anxious for the speech tomorrow. And being on the road these past weeks hasn't helped."

"Better get used to it. I've had inquiries for an even bigger tour when your next book comes out. San Francisco for sure, and St. Louis, and New York City ... it will have to be a month at least. You'll take the States by storm." He clapped Owen on the back.

Owen nodded. What on earth was the matter with him? If a genie had popped out of a bottle and asked him to make a wish, this was exactly what he would have asked for. When he'd first moved to Vancouver, he'd written a list of milestones that he wanted to achieve and put it in his wallet. Write a best seller. Become a member of the Hotel Vancouver's gentleman's club. Give a keynote speech at the British Columbian Naturalist Society.

Seemingly overnight, it had all been handed to him on a platter. Wealthy and powerful men invited him to dinner. He was traveling across the country, and people were paying to listen to his ideas. Hell, Parliament was even paying attention. Beautiful women asked for his autograph. His books were all sold out, and he'd recently signed a contract for a non-fiction book about the conservation movement. It was all happening, and yet he felt so bored and unsettled.

After their novelty had worn off, the sparkling dinner parties had increasingly felt like a competition in which each person tried to insert the wittiest observation into the discussion. He felt as if he were attending a play, not having a conversation with real people. More and more, he found himself taking off on hiking expeditions just to avoid being Owen Sterling, Celebrated Hero.

A small chime sounded, and the room quieted. Yes, it was *exactly* like being at a play. The president of the Naturalist Society walked to the front of the room.

"Ladies and gentlemen, thank you so much for coming tonight. I am pleased to inform you that tonight's lecture marks our highest attendance yet. I won't bore you with the usual introductions, since the man who is speaking tonight needs no introduction. He is here to tell you about his research on the migratory patterns of wolves in advance of his big speech in Parliament tomorrow, but I'm sure he will be happy to answer questions about his other, more thrilling, areas of expertise." A ripple of polite laughter washed through the room. "Please join me in welcoming to the lectern Mr. Owen Sterling."

Owen gave his talk. Everyone did a very good impression of listening, but when the talk was over, not one question was about wolves.

"Mr. Sterling, could you recount for us the tale of your heroic rescue?"

"Mr. Sterling, is it true that you may buy property soon? And if so, is this a sign that you might soon take a wife?"

"Mr. Sterling, if you are remaining in town over the weekend, should we expect you at the Orphans' Aid Society Fundraising Gala next week? We would very much love for you to attend."

He answered their questions as best he could and retreated to the back of the room as the standing ovation continued.

"They loved you!" Dubs thumped him on the back. "I need to introduce you to two or three people, and then we can go and toast your success."

"Actually," Owen said, "I think I'm coming down with a cold. I'm heading back to the hotel. Must protect the speaking voice, you know."

Before Dubs could react, Owen was out the door and into the cool autumn night. The Ottawa air was dry, tinged with coal smoke and burning leaves. He found himself wishing for some humidity, the faint tang of minerals in the breeze ...

What on earth was he doing, ducking out early? He would almost certainly have benefited by meeting with the people Dubs had wanted to introduce him to. He was throwing away his good fortune. For fifteen years, he'd tried to work his way into the company of the great and the good, but a few days in Fraser Springs seemed to have stripped away all the polish he'd painstakingly applied to his manners. Doc and Nils hadn't even known his real name, yet in one week he'd had more genuine conversations with them than he had ever had in Vancouver. Was it worth feeling like an imposter simply to get a chance to turn himself into a pale imitation of Dubs? To receive an invitation to the Orphans' Aid Society Fundraising Gala?

And then there was Jo. He thought about her, dreamed of her, caught himself staring at slim, auburn-haired women to see if they had her grey eyes. He'd made an effort to talk to the first few young ladies he'd been introduced to in Vancouver. But he'd quickly realized he was judging all of them against Jo, and none ever measured up. And how could they? Jo ran her own business. She could hold her own against any man, himself included. These girls seemed to think sitting through a single lecture or making dinner party small talk about the weather would impress him.

He was checking off every item on his list of what success would look like, and it felt empty. He could buy that big house in the West End, but who would live in it with him? Lord, he had been so stupid. He had walked away from Jo, insulted her to her face. He couldn't blame her for wanting nothing more to do with him; she hadn't even acknowledged the window glass that he'd sent as a peace offering. He'd told her that he didn't want to be pen pals, but even the most impersonal letter from her would have felt like a gift. Doc Stryker had warned him that she was proud and protective of her independence, and he simply hadn't listened. And now his life stretched out before him in an endless parade of roast beef dinners, smoky parlours, and ice cream shaped like swans.

He was so distracted by these gloomy thoughts that he didn't even notice that he had arrived back at the hotel. When he stopped at the front desk to get his key, the clerk handed him a stack of mail with Vancouver postmarks. His correspondence caught up with him in fits and starts on this tour. He flipped through the envelopes. A bill or two, some heavy stationery that obviously contained formal invitations of one kind or another, a packet from his clipping service ... and a long, thin envelope that bore *her* tidily handwritten name in the return address.

The weariness of the day evaporated instantly. He practically ran up the stairs to his room, ripped open the envelope, and began to read.

Dear Owen,

As I write this, I am staring out the window you sent. It is so wonderful to have the parlour filled with light again. I don't know how to thank you for such an extravagant gift.

Your article has caused such a stir. Mrs. McSheen is reveling in her role in the whole affair. I half believe the rumour that she is having her letter to the editor engraved on a plaque. Business at the bathhouse has tripled, at least—you would laugh yourself silly to hear the polite city folk gushing about the "authentic wilderness experience" they are having. Doc Stryker will be offering his own "authentic wilderness experience" again soon, as the Society Ladies have been fundraising to rebuild his bar. I never thought I'd see the day.

I am no good at these types of letters. Apologies have never been my strong suit. I am sorry, Owen. You accused me of cowardice, and I was so deeply offended. But you were right. After Albert died, I nearly lost everything. I sold my wedding ring. For two years I was a week away from bankruptcy. I know that I don't have the courage to start from nothing again. So I panicked. I pushed you away.

The window is the most beautiful, thoughtful gift that anyone has ever given me, and it makes me suspect that you listened when I tried to explain what's important to me.

You asked me if I needed you (even if you were an ass in the way you asked it). I've thought about very little except that question since you left. I understand that my life here is not the kind of life that you want for yourself, and I still don't think I can bear to uproot myself, even for you. But I love you, Owen. You fill my thoughts, my dreams, and I'm half sick with wanting you to walk through my door again. I tried to explain it away as infatuation, but the fact is that I can no longer imagine sharing my life, my work, my bed with anyone except you.

I don't know what I'm expecting by sending this letter. Please write me back.

Love,

Jo

Owen carefully folded the letter back up into thirds then unfolded it to read over again. He poured himself a drink then sat back down on the bed to read the letter a third time. Jo missed him. She thought about him all the time. She was swallowing her pride to tell him that she needed him after all. She *loved* him. He traced his fingers over the "I love you" inscribed on the paper. She'd actually written the words.

His first instinct was to run the entire way to Fraser Springs in his shirtsleeves. But what would he do after he got there? Or at least, what would he do after he found Jo and kissed her senseless? Acting like an impulsive fool is what had spooked her in the first place. He needed to let her know that she could depend on him. He needed a plan.

Late into the night, he scrawled dates and places and schedules and then crossed them out to begin again. Damn, the letter was already three weeks old. Time was not on his side, but estranging powerful people from Ottawa to Halifax by canceling the remainder of his tour didn't make sense either. Just because Jo didn't need him to be Vancouver's Most Eligible Bachelor didn't mean that he should throw the opportunity away completely. If he could turn this tour into another advance, he could arrive in Fraser Springs with a beautiful engagement ring in his pocket and enough money to last out the winter.

Two more weeks until the tour was over. He'd be back in BC in time for Thanksgiving. He'd have to give notice to his landlady, settle his accounts at his favourite restaurants and shops, take a day or two to pack. He looked around the sparse hotel room. Strike that last one. Everything he needed was already waiting for him in Fraser Springs.

Chapter 30

Autumn was lovely in Fraser Springs. Jo and Ilsa hurried through one of the last items on the evening's long list of tasks: repairing the pine garlands that festooned the bathhouse windows. They'd fallen during last night's windstorm, and the wooden walkway outside the bathhouse was littered with green needles. With thirty guests arriving soon for their Thanksgiving party, everything had to look perfect. Already, the bathhouse smelled gloriously of roasting pork and wine mulled in cranberries, nutmeg, and cinnamon sticks.

"Ouch!" Ilsa said. "You keep dropping these, and my hands are going to look like pincushions."

"Sorry," Jo said, snapping out of her reverie enough to hoist the garland higher so that Ilsa could secure it to the window with a red bow.

Ilsa sucked her sore thumb and shrugged. "Might send Nils for some cedar branches. They'll smell lovely among the candles tonight." She smiled. "Shall we also hang some mistletoe?"

Jo smirked at her. "That's Christmas, and you know it. *And* after all the work we've done scrubbing this place's reputation, you want to bring the scourge of chaste kissing to our door?"

Ilsa laughed. Her cheeks were pink from exertion, and the rich light of sunset falling on her blond ringlets made her look like she belonged in a church's window or on a Valentine's card. A small flurry of red and gold leaves spangled the air around the women. In winter, the hot springs would cast a haze about the town, smudging everyone's silhouettes and wrapping the mountains in a thin gauze. The little shacks nestled in the hills would be invisible save for the wispy spires of smoke from their chimneys.

"You got your eye on someone?" Jo teased. "I'll be happy to hang the mistletoe on your account."

"In this town? Not unless a boatload of handsome strangers comes to our door tonight. Ah, well. I'll hang it on the back porch where it won't do much harm. Maybe it will still bring some luck, even if it's out of season."

Off in the distance, the low hoot of the SS *Minto* announced its arrival. Ilsa stared towards the lake, trying to make out the ship.

Jo touched her friend's shoulder to retrieve her attention. "Come on. No time for daydreaming!"

Together, they spent the next few hours preparing vast quantities of food, nestling the fragrant evergreen boughs among the candles, polishing the silver, and setting the good linens along the table. Soon, the sun was setting, and Jo went upstairs to change her outfit.

Her one formal gown was pressed and lay on her bed. The emerald grosgrain silk had held up well in the years since her wedding. The dress had been a gift from Albert; it had arrived in a beribboned box tucked among layer after layer of tissue paper. It was the prettiest thing she had ever owned, and even now, she could recall the way Albert had looked at her as they'd stood at the altar.

Jo undressed, then filled the basin with water. The warped mirror distorted the reflection of her body, lengthening and widening it depending on how she moved, but still she stared at herself, trying to see what Owen had seen. Cold air summoned goose bumps along her thighs, her arms, the tops of her breasts, coaxing up the fine hairs on her arms and legs, just as they had when she had stepped out of the pool and the water had sluiced off her and Owen had taken her in his arms and—

Enough. She moved away briskly. No sense torturing herself with memories like that. She applied some scent behind her ears then laced her corset. It had been years since she'd worn one. The stays chafed against her own rib bones: the only good thing about wearing a corset was taking it off.

Jo picked up the gown, surprised by its weight. She held it up to the window and the emerald silk seemed to faintly glow, a stark contrast to the mist and the creeping darkness. After years of wearing serviceable, practical clothing, the crinolines and petticoats felt as heavy as pig iron as she put them on. Though she was glad to finally be in the good books of the Fraser Springs hostesses, she was not looking forward to an evening of trying to remember the dance steps of her youth while weighed down by an extra twenty pounds of dress.

Cheer up. If the worst thing that happens to you is that you have to wear a pretty dress, you're not that badly off, are you? No one was wrapping letters around bricks. No one was trying to run her out of town. She should at least try to greet the evening with a happy face.

She practiced that happy face in the mirror. She fixed the smile with dash of colour from the rouge pot, pinched her cheeks, affixed the tortoiseshell comb to the side of her chignon, and studied the results. The dress smelled of the pine box it had been stored in, the scent reminding her of the woods she loved and the grotto that was her one safe place in the world. No, her life was not so bad. She had so much, and yet ...

A knock at the door announced the first guest's arrival. She gave herself one last inspection in the mirror and headed downstairs to greet her visitor.

"Why hello, my dear, dear Mrs. Wilson!" Mrs. McSheen cried. Her dress had so many crinolines that she seemed to take up half of the dining room. As she walked, she listed side to side like a gigantic church bell. "A happy Thanksgiving to you! I know I'm the slightest bit early, but I wanted to come and make sure that you weren't running into any difficulty. I should certainly know that hosting can be a challenge, especially with this many people. Why, when I threw my famous New Year's party of '07, people kept coming up to me and saying, 'My dearest, I don't know how you managed to pull it off without falling over from exhaustion.'"

"A happy Thanksgiving to you too," Jo said, kissing the woman's cheeks. Her liberal application of perfume blasted away the comforting smells of roast pork and evergreen. "And how lovely you look! May I offer you some punch?"

Mrs. McSheen paused to consider this. "I shouldn't, but it's a special occasion, so I suppose it would be in poor taste not to partake." She gave a dramatic sigh.

Ilsa poured Mrs. McSheen a glass of punch, and Jo tried very hard to nod at the appropriate moments in the litany of McSheen family illnesses and misfortunes. Soon, however, the door rang again. Doc Stryker was wearing a crushed velvet suit of indeterminate vintage— a little threadbare at the elbows but still in excellent condition—and he carried a carved wooden cane in one hand and a jug of beer in the other. Since the destruction of his precious still, Doc Stryker had switched to beer. Hops grew wild in these parts, and it would be months, he said, until his new batch of hooch reached the critical potency.

All the girls stopped what they were doing to greet him.

"Ladies!" Doc said, grinning widely. "No need to fight over me. There's plenty of the old man to go around." He winked at Jo. "It's the suit that does it. Drives the ladies wild. Why, I've been charming gals in this suit since before you all were even thought of."

He handed over the jug then took Ilsa by the arm. "Now. You'll all be happy to know that I've come in good time to sample the roast to ensure that it's of the highest quality. Not that I would ever doubt you, my dear Ilsa, but one can never be too careful.

Even the finest chef can benefit from an impartial palate." She patted his hand, and together they strode off to the kitchen.

More guests arrived, and the room filled up with the rustle of taffeta skirts, the shriek of knives on china, and happy chatter. A group had assembled by the piano, and everyone was taking turns half remembering the lyrics of carols. It didn't seem to matter what the words actually were or what language they were in. Nils dipped in and out of Danish. Someone else sang in Gaelic. The pianist kept up, and everyone clapped along. Ilsa and Nils danced a jig in the middle of a circle of stomping people, and suddenly everyone was swinging their partners around so that the room seemed to tilt dizzily with the rhythm of the twirling bodies.

Jo leaned against the wall with a small glass of punch in her hands and watched the skirts of every colour seem to blend and swirl together. She closed her eyes. The warmth of the music and the alcohol diffused through her limbs. A good night. For the first time in months, she felt grateful for what she had, instead of spending her time focusing on what she'd lost.

Her thoughts were interrupted by Ilsa slinging her arms around her. "It's hot in here. Let's get some air." She was breathless from dancing and high spirits, as happy as Jo had ever seen her.

Jo smiled back. Together, they wove their way through the dancers and out into the sharp air and silence of the back porch. It was much cooler outside, and a brisk breeze blew down from the mountains. Jo closed her eyes again to listen to the soft rustle of the leaves collecting in drifts among the trees and the buildings, and the lapping water of the gently steaming lake. The crunch of shoes in the fallen leaves made her open her eyes.

She started to remark to Ilsa that they needed to head back inside, but the person standing in front of her wasn't Ilsa.

"Hi," Owen said. The warm, golden light of the porch lamp made his sandy hair glow.

"How did you—?" She looked around. He seemed to have magically appeared out of the ether. In one hand, he held a suitcase. In the other, a folded piece of paper. "How long have you been out here?"

Owen smiled sheepishly. "Maybe a half hour. Ilsa certainly took her time. I was beginning to think that she was going to let me starve to death on your doorstep just to teach me a lesson." He gestured to her dress. "You look beautiful, by the way."

Jo took a few steps towards him. She touched his face. He was back. He was here. Somehow, he was really here. "Oh, my God. Come in. Come in!" She reached for his hand, only to bump against the suitcase he was still carrying.

"Wait," he said. "I have something for you. It's taken me so long to respond to your letter that I thought I'd better hand-deliver mine." He set the suitcase down and held out the piece of folded paper in his other hand. She took the paper from his— trembling?— fingers.

Despite her sudden clumsiness, she unfolded the letter. It bore only two words: *Look down*. And there, on her kitchen porch, was Owen Sterling on one knee. Her hands flew to cover her gasp and stayed there, pressing against her lips.

"You are the most astonishing woman I've ever met," he said. His hair was askew with the breeze, and his cheeks were pink with cold, giving him an almost boyish look. And that expression: she'd been dreaming of that expression in the long months since he'd left. "You're smart, and beautiful, and brave enough to know what you want and to fight for it. I'm so, so sorry it took me so long to realize that you're what I want." Even in this serious moment, his eyes contained so much humour and warmth. "Because you're the only thing I want, Jo. I don't need a big house or a motorcar or the club memberships as long as I can have you. I should never have run away from you over a single disagreement, and if you can forgive me for that, I swear that I will never leave your side again.

Because I love you." For once, her inner chorus of worries and constraints was silent. All of her "what ifs?" vanished. And there, between Owen's fingers, an opal ring shimmered in the faint light. More magic. "Will you marry me?"

"Yes," she whispered, finally lowering her hands to rest on Owen's broad shoulders. He surged to his feet, guided the ring on to her left hand, and captured her in a deep kiss before she had a chance to say another word.

In the distance, she registered that her party guests were watching from her windows, clapping and cheering, but they seemed a million miles away. He kissed her, and she kissed him back, and their bodies fit against each other as if there had never been a separation.

Finally, he pulled away to give a showman's wave to the crowd streaming out of the bathhouse to surround them. Last among them was Doc Stryker, who muscled his way between them and clapped Owen on the shoulders.

"Good on you, lad," he said, grinning broadly. "See what happens when you listen to old Doc Stryker?" His eyes drifted up. "A lovely betrothal. And under the mistletoe, no less."

Jo hugged Ilsa. Her friend's blue eyes were brimming with tears. "You minx," she said. "What else have you been hiding?"

"Drinks are on me!" Doc exclaimed to universal approval.

Owen and Jo emerged from the chill of the night into the parlour, which was heavy with the scent of punch and cigar smoke and pine boughs and guttering candles, all edged with the constant mineral tang of the springs. Everyone shook their hands. Everyone asked to see the ring. Finally, drinks dispensed, Doc Stryker let out a whoop and rushed over to hug the pair once more. Jo hadn't seen him move so fast since the fire.

"What did I tell you, my lad?" he told Owen.

Owen smiled. "I've lived long enough to know that when a barkeep gives advice, it's best to heed it."

"A barkeep *and* a doctor. And it's times like this that make me miss that bottle of port I had tucked away behind my bar for special occasions. Ah, no matter." He hobbled back over to the punch bowl and poured a generous drink for both of them. "This ladies' brew will have to do. To the happy couple!"

Everyone raised their glasses in a noisy, disorganized cheer.

"To the happy couple!"

"To Owen and Jo!"

"Where will you be spending the night?" Mrs. McSheen piped up. The crowd fell silent. "Obviously, for you to stay here would be out of the question. I'm positive, however, that I can arrange a special rate for you at the St. Alice. They speak so highly of you there."

"Oh, come off it, woman," said Doc. "Let the young people be. They're too old for chaperones." He winked at Mrs. McSheen. She recoiled in horror but read the mood of the room and wisely held her tongue.

And with that, Jo and Owen were surrounded by other, slightly less genteel congratulations and suggestions. Finally, Owen took her hand, and they slipped away into the relative privacy of the kitchen. For a moment, they simply stood facing one another, holding hands. She could not believe that he was so near, that the blue eyes she had spent so much time imagining were staring straight at her.

"I should kiss you," she murmured.

"Now, now," he said, running his thumb along the top of her hand: the gesture that sent a flush of heat down into her abdomen. "What would Mrs. McSheen say?"

Jo laughed. Owen laughed too and bent down to kiss her smiling lips. "Are you sure you'd be all right with my moving in with you? We can think of something else, if you want."

She smiled. "No more thinking. I've spent so long making this complicated, but it's actually very simple. I love you. I love this place. If you're willing, I'm happy. I ... oh, Owen, I've never been so happy."

"Well then," he said, folding her into his arms. "That's settled."

And it was.

About The Author

Laine Ferndale teaches literature and writing to pay for a fairly serious chai latte habit. She began writing romance novels in graduate school; *The Scandalous Mrs. Wilson*, inspired by her honeymoon in the historic spa town of Hot Springs, Arkansas, is her first book. She lives with her husband and her adorably needy cat.